DODIE SMITH

The Midnight Kittens

CATNIP BOOKS
Published by Catnip Publishing Ltd
14 Greville Street
London EC1N 8SB

First published by W.H. Allen 1978
This edition first published 2012
1 3 5 7 9 10 8 6 4 2

A CIP catalogue record for this book is available from the British
Library

ISBN 978-1-84647-153-7

Printed in India by Replika Press

www.catnippublishing.co.uk

The
Midnight
Kittens

CONTENTS

1. ARRIVAL BY NIGHT

It was the first time the twins had made the journey by night, also the first time they had made it on their own. Usually, in their half-term holidays, they travelled from school with the children bound for London, and someone made sure they got off at the country station where their grandmother would be waiting for them. But this summer half term they had spent the first day in London, seeing art galleries and a play. And it had been decided that, now they were ten, they could be put on the train at Liverpool Street and be relied on to get off at the right station. That is, Tom could be relied on. Pamela could almost certainly be relied on to go past the station.

No one could have guessed them to be twins.

Tom, the elder by twenty minutes, had dark hair which, however hacked, somehow ended up by making a close-fitting cap for his head. His face was round, his cheeks rosy, and he was sturdily built. His headmaster (who liked his pupils to call him Mike; it was that kind of school) had once described him as 'a wonderfully good all-purpose boy'.

Pamela had long, straight, very fair hair which veiled each side of her face and made it look thinner than it was. Her skin was pale and her large, grey-blue eyes often looked woebegone when she was merely indulging in what Tom called one of her daylight dreams. Mike had once said that she looked like a child mermaid.

Pamela admired Tom's reliability but had no wish to be reliable. Tom officially disapproved of Pam's dreaminess, but was secretly wistful of it because it seemed to be tied up with imagination. Pamela was credited with having a great deal of imagination. Tom thought he had more imagination than he was credited with.

After they had been on the train for almost an hour Tom began to feel anxious. He noticed that the country stations were very badly lit; they went through several without his being able to see their names. He knew the train would *stop* at their station, but suppose he got Pam off at some earlier one? He had been told the journey would take little over an hour. He must now concentrate fiercely.

And at that moment Pam began to talk volubly. Did he remember when they had first come to live with Gram? They had changed into a train with no corridors. There had been a fascinating little engine – 'surely you remember, Tom?'

'Don't distract me,' said Tom, gazing at a black window. 'I've got to get us off at our station.' Of course he remembered the little railway line, closed years ago, and always felt sad when, on a walk, they saw its overgrown track.

They were slowing down. 'Is this us?' said Pam. 'Oh, come on quickly.' Already she was imagining being carried on into deepest Suffolk.

They could see lights now, but no station name. Tom said, 'We'll get to the door, anyway. No, let me go first.' He pushed past her knowing she was capable of flinging the door open before the train stopped and jumping out into the night.

There was a tremendous jerk. They had stopped.

'Horrid train,' said Pam, who had bumped her shoulder.

Tom had trouble in getting the door open, then got out carefully and carefully helped Pam down. He still couldn't see the name of the station. But far along the platform he could see Gram.

'She's there!' screamed Pam. 'Race you.'

Tom won and was one hug ahead of Pam.

'Oh, darlings, darlings,' said Gram. 'I've been worrying in case you got off at the wrong station.'

'No fear of that,' said Tom.

'Have you had a good day?'

'Pretty good,' said Pam. 'Some of the paintings were lovely. But the play was silly. Of course, it was intended for children.'

'Mike says he'll start us on Shakespeare next time,' said Tom.

'Did you tell him *I* started you on Shakespeare, in the Christmas holidays?'

'Well, no,' said Tom. 'He might have thought I was being superior.'

'Quite right,' said Gram, approving Tom's good manners, but a mite peeved not to have had the credit.

They clung to her as they made their way out of the station. It was larger than the stations on the little closed branch line, but very old-fashioned and dimly lit. There were no porters and the ticket office was now closed.

'Oh, good, you've got the car open,' said Tom.

She had exchanged her comfortable car for an expensive, though far from new, convertible which the twins had hankered for. And really she had quite got to like it; one could always wrap up.

'I've brought coats, and a headscarf for you, Pam, so your hair won't go mad. Mine doesn't mind the wind.'

'You've had it cut differently,' said Pam. 'Lovely.'

'Yes, the girl in the village cuts quite well.' But the truth was that Gram's hair, dark like Tom's, shared his hair's knack of looking well whoever cut it. Indeed, as regards both appearance and temperament, she might well have been described as a wonderfully good all-purpose woman.

'It's softer than your last style,' said Pam.

'You don't think it's too young for me?'

Tom said, 'Do you know what Tim Johnson said about you, when you came down before Easter?'

Tim Johnson? The head boy, Gram remembered, and prepared to be impressed.

'He said to me, "Your mother's a jolly pretty woman."'

'Your *mother*? Oh, I *love* Tim Johnson.'

They were in the car now, all in the front seats.

'I'm glad there's a moon,' said Pam.

'Yes, it's almost full,' said Gram. 'I was wondering if you'd like to climb the Bump and look around.'

'Oh, *yes*,' said both the twins.

They drove out of the station yard and through the nearby little town.

'How empty the streets are,' said Pam. 'It's as if the past has come back. Perhaps we shall see Herrick's bellman saying, "Mercie secure ye all, and keep the Goblin from ye, while ye sleep." '

Once they were through the town they drove past the park of a large estate, where the shadows of great trees were black on the grass. Then they were in farming country.

'I wish they wouldn't cut down so many hedges,' said Tom. 'Oh, I know the reason but Mike says it's often short-sighted. If you cut down the birds' homes there are no birds to eat the insects and then you have to depend on foul insecticides – oh, I'm sorry, Gram.'

'I thought Mike was trying to outlaw swearing.'

'Well, he is but he doesn't absolutely forbid it in case it drives it underground.'

'Like drugs,' said Pam.

'Don't tell me Mike's got a drug problem.'

'If so, it hasn't come our way,' said Tom. 'Of course, we're a bit young to attract pushers.'

'Anyway, we've *honour* promised you,' said Pam. 'And about smoking.'

Gram thought of all the years she herself had smoked. She had given it up when she inherited the twins. 'One cannot,' she had once said, 'puff smoke in a baby's face.' Had she smoked when their father was a baby? Only very occasionally; the habit had grown on her during the war, and more and more after her husband's death.

'There's the Bump,' cried Tom.

It had originally been the base of a castle keep, of which no stone now remained – to the regret of the twins; they loved ruins. Now there was only a grassy mound; Pam had once said it looked like a giant's overturned pudding basin. It rose from one of the few remaining meadows of their much-cultivated countryside.

They got out of the car and climbed a gate. Gram was a nifty gate-climber but she still wished there were more stiles. What had happened to stiles? And there weren't many wishing gates left, either.

'Race you to the top,' said Tom as they neared the mound.

It was a dead heat for the twins, with Gram only a few yards behind.

'And she's not a bit puffed,' said Pam.

Gram would have burst rather than show signs of being puffed. Good heavens, one was only in one's . . . well, fairly late fifties. And one kept a careful eye on the bathroom scales.

She had brought a mac to spread on the grass; there was a heavy dew. They sat close together.

'This is the first time we've been up here by moonlight,' said Pam. 'I wonder if we can see as much as by day.'

First they located Himbers. (The origin of that name had been forgotten locally even when Gram and her husband first found the house back in the 1930s. The twins always thought of their grandfather as 'Gram's husband'. He had died before they were born and they never had any sense of being related to him. And as their mother's parents were dead also, they had no grandfather at all. Pam had once said, 'We really are very fully orphaned, aren't we? But Gram makes up for everything.')

'Oh, the garden lights are on!' said Tom.

'That's to welcome you,' said Gram. She no longer had them on every night. One must make what little economies one could.

Pam said, 'Strange, seeing that the moon's so bright, that one can't see much detail; only masses, silver and black. The front garden, the orchard – how the pond gleams! And the paddock. You don't feel the need of ponies to eat the paddock grass?'

'Well, not just yet.' Gram wondered if the twins now felt the need for ponies. It would take more than little economies to pay for those. 'Some farmer's always willing to cut it for the hay.'

'Hay's extremely expensive now,' said Tom. 'Perhaps you should sell it.'

'I hardly like to, after so many years. But it's a bright idea, Tom.'

His gaze was already travelling further afield. 'There are more hedges than I expected. I suppose they keep growing again.'

'Yes, hedges are very forgiving,' said Gram. 'Unless they're actually rooted out.'

Pam said, 'I love so many of the fields being a different shape and I specially love the little fields and the little bits of woods. It's a wonder farmers leave those – or even any trees. How mysterious

Freke Hall looks by moonlight.'

'It looks pretty mysterious by daylight,' said Tom.

'It won't for much longer,' said Gram. 'It's going to be put in good order and opened up.'

The twins turned to her eagerly. 'Does that mean the missing heir's turned up?' said Pam.

'He wasn't really missing, just unwilling; a whole series of him, I believe, somewhere in Australia. None of them wanted to live in Freke Hall. But now it's been sold – or perhaps let on a long lease; no one in the village knows the rights of it. Anyway, it's going to be used by a firm of antique dealers who'll display their furniture there.'

'I don't think I like that,' said Pam. 'It'll be like turning it into a shop.'

'Well, it'll be better than letting it go on mouldering away,' said Tom.

'It hasn't exactly mouldered,' said Gram. 'There's been enough money to keep the outside in repair, specially the roof. Once the roof goes, a house dies. *I* like the idea of the fine rooms being filled with fine furniture.'

'But the furniture will always be moving on,' said Pam. 'It'll never *live* in the house. Anyway, I wish I could have seen inside before it's all done up.'

'You're going to,' said Gram. 'The vicar arranged for it to be open to the public for a couple of weeks, in aid of the church. Tomorrow's the last day. I've resisted the temptation to go on my own, so that we could all see it together.'

'Oh, wonderful,' said Pam.

'Strange I've never had the chance to go inside. It had been closed for quite a number of years when your grandfather and I first came here. But the gardens weren't quite overgrown then. We used to wander round and peer through the windows.'

'We were never able to do that,' said Tom, 'because they were so overgrown with bushes and creepers.'

'I'm told they've already got rid of lots of those and cleaned up inside. But it'll take months to cope with the plumbing and repairs and decorations.'

'I almost wish they'd let it alone,' said Pam. 'The *thought* of it used to be thrilling. Still, it'll be fun to see inside. And thank you for waiting to see it with us. You *are* kind. Tom, let's join up and give Gram something to lean on.'

They moved closer and stretched their arms behind their grandmother, gripping her shoulders.

'Now lean back into your chair,' said Tom.

'*Most* comfortable,' said Gram, untruthfully.

Pam, gazing up at the sky, said, 'Oh, I do like being us.'

'Me, too,' said Tom.

'And me, too,' echoed Gram, fervently. And, as so often at moments of happiness shared with them, felt a pang of something like guilt. She could never feel quite sure she had the right to her full share in their lives, when their poor young parents had barely had a share at all. It was some comfort to know that, killed instantaneously on a continental motorway, they could not have had time to know all they were losing.

And Gram knew that, could they have realised they were about to die, what would have mattered most to them would not have been the loss of a life shared with their children, but the loss of a life shared with each other. They were so young. They had not planned to have children so soon. But they were on their way to accepting their responsibility. That fatal continental holiday was to have been their last until the twins were old enough to come with them.

Over nine years and there was rarely a day when she did not remember it. But she never allowed herself to think about it for long when she was with the twins in case some of her unhappiness somehow got through to them. But *was* she unhappy any longer? Perhaps it was her happiness that made her feel guilty.

She said now, 'How peaceful it is. We're lucky that our countryside's so unspoilt.'

There was a sudden roaring in the sky. She felt Pam clutch her shoulder and said reassuringly, 'It's only a plane.'

Pam, who had merely been startled, said, 'If we were back in the Middle Ages we'd be terrified by that noise.'

'Even only a hundred years ago we would have been,' said Tom.

Pam tried to summon up a little delicious terror. 'We don't actually know it's a plane.'

'What else could it be?' said Tom, satirically. 'A flying saucer?'

'Oh, *no*. UFOs are dreary. But it could be a dragon. That's just the kind of noise a dragon with powerful wings would make.'

Now the plane's coloured lights were visible.

'It's a very smart dragon,' said Tom. 'All dressed up like a Christmas tree. I wonder where the idea of dragons came from, seeing that they never existed.'

'Of course they existed. In the age of magic.'

'When *was* that, Pam?' asked her grandmother.

'No one knows now, because people have stopped believing in it. Of course, it's still there, ready to be believed in.'

'Aren't you being a bit fancy?' said Tom.

'Certainly not. Actually, magic's coming back already. How about ESP, telepathy, and so on?'

'There's a scientific explanation of those – well, sort of.' He was already annoyed with himself for calling Pam fancy. He felt he had been stodgy.

Gram said, 'I think magic's very much linked with

imagination. Pam has so much of that. Perhaps girls are more imaginative than boys.'

'Boys have imagination too,' said Tom. 'How about Shakespeare?'

Gram laughed. 'You win, Tom. Well, home to supper now. And don't run down the mound and end by falling.'

They usually did run and they usually did end by falling, but tonight they went sedately. Hurtling downwards would have shattered the moonlit peace.

Back in the car Gram asked if they wanted to drive through the village – 'or are you too hungry?'

They decided they were.

'Anyway, the village by night isn't what it used to be,' said Gram, 'now the pub dresses itself up in neon lights.'

So they skirted the village and soon sighted the four tall poplars which stood outside the white wood fence of Himbers, their tips silvered by moonlight. Gram put the car in the garage that had once been a stable and then the three of them walked towards the garden gate.

'Oh, wait, wait,' cried Pam. 'Let's take in the house all lit up, with the curtains drawn back.'

'I thought you'd like that,' said Gram.

Tom said, 'I love the way the dining room and the sitting room look like one big room, because you can't see the fireplaces, and the book shelves in the back wall seem to run right the way through.'

'Fascinating,' said Pam. 'It's almost like coming to a different house. Not that I'd want it to be a different house, but it's fun that it can be two houses at once.'

Tom opened the white wooden gate and they went into the long front garden.

2. HIMBERS

'What smells so sweet?' asked Pam.

'The tobacco plant – and there's some night-scented stock.' Gram sighed. 'I really ought to have the herbaceous borders turfed. The garden's getting too much for Hildy, though I help him all I can.'

'Will he be waiting up for us?' said Tom.

'I asked him not to.' Gram glanced towards a cottage on the edge of the paddock. 'His light's still on but at least he's off duty. He was tired tonight because he'd been mowing the orchard grass in your honour. Of course he has a good motor-mower but you do have to walk with them.'

'What he needs', said Pam, 'is one of those mowers you ride on.'

'Yes, indeed. I've been thinking that.' Gram had also been thinking of the cost. Such things, including ponies, could not be bought out of income, and this was no moment to sell any of her investments. 'He really does too much, what with helping in the house, but he doesn't like the idea of getting rid of any of his flower beds, and one does have to be careful not to make old people feel old.'

Twenty years earlier, Mr and Mrs Hilditch had come to Himbers as gardener and cook-housekeeper. No longer young, they had been glad of a quiet job in the country and they had proved to be blessings Gram had never ceased to be grateful for, especially during that dreadful year when her husband had died and, only a few months later, the twins' parents had been killed. She had wondered if she should leave Himbers but, once she became guardian of the twins, she had wanted to bring them up there. A new era of growing content had begun. Then, five years ago, Mrs Hilditch, who was older than her husband, had died and he had quite wonderfully helped to take her place, even doing some of the cooking. Not for anything would Gram have done without him and she knew he could not bear to be done without. But she did sometimes wonder how long he could carry on; he was well into his seventies. But he had been a strong man and she considered herself to be a fairly strong woman. They could certainly carry on for the present.

'Do you think he ever feels lonely?' said Pam, as they walked up the long, brick path towards the white, red-tiled old house.

'Not when he's working in the garden – he once said, "A garden's wonderful company." And we always have our meals together now, though he still insists on waiting on me all he can. And he has good friends in the village. Oh, I think Hildy's happy enough, bless him.' She opened the front door and switched the garden lights off. There was one at each corner of the house.

The front door opened straight into the dining room. 'The fire's out,' wailed Pam, with one of her sudden plunges into dismay.

'Oh dear, and I lit it specially to welcome you,' said Gram.

'It is *not* out,' said Tom, who had long ago decided that neither his sister nor his grandmother were good at coping with wood fires. 'I'll have it blazing up the chimney in a minute.' He seized the bellows and knelt down on the wide, open hearth.

'Not too much,' said Gram. 'We haven't really needed fires for weeks. We'll get the supper, Pam.'

By the time they returned Tom had the fire blazing but had been judicious with logs. 'These two thin ones will last until we go to bed.' He surveyed the table with satisfaction. 'My very favourite meal. Soup, sandwiches, chocolate cake and milk in a huge jug, not just mugs of it. Not that I mind mugs but with a jug you can go on pouring out more and more.'

'Don't you ever get soup and sandwiches at school?'

'Well, the soup's in open soup plates, never in lovely brown pots with lids; and it's usually thin, with things floating in it.' Tom lifted the lid off his soup. 'Oh, thick *white* soup – specially good.'

Pam said, 'As for sandwiches, we only get them for outings and they're usually a bit door-steppy. Not that Mike doesn't give us very good food on the whole. You couldn't cut sandwiches like these for a whole school.'

'Are you having a good term?'

'Even better than usual,' said Tom. 'We've been having more lessons with Mike.'

'Mike's wonderful,' said Pam. 'He's got a new thing now, called Midnight Oil Sessions, for children who are miserable about, well, anything, though it's usually their home life; parents are *shocking*, specially the rich ones. Mike's busy all day – of course he works at night, too, but he's on his own then; it's such a good thing he's not married. And he lets children book appointments to talk to him. He's often talking to them after midnight.'

'Does he let them sit up as late as that?'

'He says it's better than that they should lie awake brooding, when things get too much for them. Of course he starts long before midnight but children go on talking. We've never had a Midnight Oil Session because we've never really had any need.' Pam sounded faintly wistful.

'Well, the more I know of Mike, the more I like him,' said Gram. She had sent the twins to his school because their mother had been there and liked it – though in the days when Mike's father had been its headmaster. It had sounded frighteningly modern to Gram but she had felt she was carrying out what might have been the wish of her poor dead daughter-in-law. And it was turning out wonderfully well. Thankful for this, Gram often told herself she must always be ready to accept the *new*. The generation gap could be bad enough between children and parents. Between children and a grandparent, it could be fatal.

Pam was continuing, 'Of course, I *could* ask for a session about my atheism, but it wouldn't be fair as I'm not really troubled.'

'I don't think I know about your atheism,' said Gram, carefully keeping her tone casual.

'Well, it's a new thing. Mike's been taking classes on Comparative Religions. Fascinating. And when we had a full discussion afterwards he decided that Tom could get away with being an agnostic, but I'd better face my atheism and give it a chance to work its way out of my system.'

Tom said, 'You ought to explain, Pam, that Mike thinks you have a fundamentally religious temperament or you wouldn't feel so strongly about the subject. Most of the children couldn't care less. They said they were C of E and didn't mind it at all.'

'I'm the only atheist in the class,' said Pam, 'and Tom's the only agnostic. There's one boy who fancies being a Buddhist. Mike's getting him some books.'

'Don't you believe in God at all?' asked Gram.

'I don't believe in a personal God.'

'If you mean the old gentleman with a long white beard sitting on a cloud, I don't think many of us believe that, nowadays,' said Gram.

'I believe in the idea of Good, which includes Love, Truth, Beauty, *everything* good. And it's within everyone – not outside, expecting to be worshipped.'

Tom said, 'Mike says the idea of Good's so hard to think about.'

'I know,' said Pam, gloomily. 'I'm beginning to see it as a vague golden lump, a bit like butter. Terribly hard to hang on to.'

'Well, butter would be,' said Tom.

They all laughed happily. Then Gram said, 'Does Mike have any religion of his own?'

'He seems to be able to believe in a whole lot of them at the same time,' said Tom. 'But he once said he thought the most important aspect of God was Truth. He's very worried about what he calls "The Decay of Truth" in the modern world. He says the time may come when people won't know what truth *is*, they'll lie without knowing they're lying.'

'It's the one thing he's strict about,' said Pam. 'He doesn't even hold with little white lies, meant to spare people's feelings – he says they don't matter in themselves but they all add to the Decay of Truth.

But he doesn't think one should be *ostentatiously* truthful. Gram, can we put the lights out and finish our supper by the fire? There'll be enough light if Tom bellows up the flames again.'

They carried their chocolate cake and milk to the fireplace where the twins, once Tom had coaxed another blaze from the logs, squatted on the hearthstone. Gram sat on the fender stool. She was pleased with herself for not showing dismay about Pam's atheism. The twins were obviously taking a more serious interest in religion than she herself had ever taken. She went to the village church fairly often and played her part in all the activities to raise money for it, but she knew her attitude was much like that of the twins' classmates who were just 'C of E and didn't really mind it at all'. Religion had not helped her when she was stricken by the deaths of her husband and her son; nothing had, until the coming of the twins.

Pam said, 'Do you remember how we used to do this on Christmas Eve, Tom, and talk about Santa Claus? I used to leave him a piece of cake.'

'I don't think I ever quite believed in him,' said Tom.

'What, not even when you were tiny?' said Gram.

'I must have told you about him when you were only two or three.'

Tom considered, 'Well, certainly not after I was four. I mean he'd have got burnt, not to mention filthy. And there was never any soot on the presents he brought.'

'But magic could have taken care of all that,' said Pam.

'I was never quite as keen on magic as you and Gram were. Of course I kept my unbelief to myself, so as not to spoil things for you both.'

'Very considerate,' said Gram. 'Though I did gradually realise you were humouring me. Pam wasn't. She was most upset when I told her the truth when she was seven.'

'Not as upset as I was when I found out fairy tales never really happened,' said Pam. 'After all, Santa Claus was only an old man, very red in the face, not at all romantic. But I still think it's awful when children are robbed of princes and princesses and fairyland generally – after we've had them for all those years.'

'Did I ever actually tell you fairy tales were true?' said Gram.

'Well, you didn't tell us they weren't. And most

of them begin, "Once upon a time there was," not "Once upon a time there wasn't." '

'I suppose I took it for granted that truth would seep through, once you'd learned to read when you were seven.'

'I never cared so much for fairy tales as Pam did,' said Tom. 'I suspect she went on believing because she wanted to.'

Pam said, 'I had so many imaginary places. There was a woodland fairyland, with the fairy queen and exquisite fairies and elves. And there was a quite different fairyland with a royal court – rather eighteenth century. And there was Nursery Rhyme Land. I was robbed of the whole lot.'

'But why couldn't you enjoy them just as stories?' asked Gram.

'Because they started off by being real to me. I couldn't go on *living* in them. Tom, can you get any more flames out of those logs?'

The logs still glowed but Tom could get nothing but sparks.

'And we must go to bed,' said Gram, getting up and switching on the lights. 'You can take the rest of the milk up with you and some more chocolate cake.' She did not remind them to clean their teeth the very last thing. It was a long established custom.

They carried out the soup cups and sandwich dishes and stacked them in Gram's little dishwasher. On the kitchen table was a large shallow bowl of bread and milk. 'That's for our hedgehogs,' said Gram.

'Oh, have we hedgehogs?' said Tom, delightedly.

'We used to have some years ago – your grandfather was particularly fond of them. Then they disappeared; I'm afraid they often get run over. But we've a fine pair now. I've been feeding them for weeks.'

'That's Mogg's old dish,' said Tom.

Mogg had been a huge black cat who had died less than a year earlier, aged well over eighteen. The twins had found it hard to believe that when she first arrived, as a young stray, she had been both thin and skittish. Their earliest memories of her were as a weighty cat who resented familiarities. Gram had adored her, all the more because her husband had, too. She had been so famous a cat locally, both for her size and age, that the Parish Magazine had given her a long obituary.

'We'll take it out through the french window,' said Gram.

Tom carried the dish through the dining room to the sitting room, where a french window opened on to the orchard.

'How lovely it looks,' said Pam, as they stepped out into the moonlight. 'I'm glad Hildy hasn't mown down all the cow parsley.'

'I like him to leave some until it looks ragged,' said Gram. There was a lacy drift of it all round the long, narrow pond except where there were some stepping-stones, much favoured by the wild ducks. And there was some round every tree. As well as old fruit trees there were chestnuts, birch, lilac and laburnum, and a willow tree overhanging the pond. And the whole orchard was enclosed by a very high hedge. The twins felt it was a wonderfully private place.

'Oh, the great white lilac's in bloom,' cried Pam. It was some way along the orchard, its whiteness seeming to claim all the moonlight for itself. It was a very special tree for them all. 'I can't wait to see it by daylight.'

'Moonlight's even better than sunlight,' said Tom.

It was the kind of remark with which, Gram thought, Tom often surprised her. She put the bread and milk down some little way from the french window. 'The hedgehogs won't come till we've gone, but if you look down from the landing window you may see them feeding. You can shine a torch down on them; they don't seem to mind torchlight. But you must keep very quiet. I meet them sometimes, when I walk in the orchard at night, and at first they just freeze into stillness; but the minute you take your eyes off them, they're gone – unbelievably fast.'

They went in and Gram bolted the french window. Then the twins got their cake and milk and they all went up to bed. The stairs led from the dining room. Himbers, a seventeenth-century farmhouse, had large rooms but not very many of them. Gram's bedroom was over the kitchen. The spare room and the bathroom were over the dining room. There had once been a very large room over the sitting room but Gram had divided it into two small bedrooms for the twins, leaving a passage between them wide enough to be a sitting room. There was room for bookcases and cupboards and a table and chairs, and there was a deep window seat at the large window which looked out over the orchard. The twins thought their passage sitting room much more interesting than most ordinary sitting rooms.

Tom put the cake and milk down on the table,

then switched the passage light off and they both knelt on the window seat, looking down into the moonlit orchard. There was no sign of the hedgehogs.

'Let's get into our dressing gowns,' said Pam.

They went into their rooms. Pam's was at the front of the house, Tom's at the back. They loved their rooms, particularly the very small washbasins across a corner of each room. Pam's was green, Tom's was yellow. Those washbasins were one reason why Gram could count on their brushing their teeth. She had laid out their dressing gowns and pyjamas on their beds. Pam's had green sheets, Tom's were yellow.

They were back on the window seat in under two minutes. Pam said, 'Gram's put honeysuckle in my room. What have you got?'

'Syringa,' said Tom. 'She really is a supergram.'

Still no hedgehogs. Tom opened the window wide, then said, 'Do you know, I've never actually seen a hedgehog?'

'Me, neither. Only in books. They have sweet little faces, though a bit witch-like; I used to think they were particularly magical animals. Have some cake.'

They ate some cake and drank some milk. Then Tom said, 'There's the village church clock striking midnight.'

It was only possible to hear it on still, silent nights as the village was almost two miles away.

'Don't interrupt it,' said Pam. When the last stroke had struck she said, 'I always want to make midnight last longer. It's the most magical time there is. But of course that doesn't mean anything to you.'

'I don't exactly not believe in magic,' said Tom. 'It's just that I don't quite know what it is. When one was little one just took it for granted but now one doesn't. Anyway, I do agree that midnight is . . . well, an impressive sort of time. If anything magical could turn up it might very well turn up then.'

'Ssh!' said Pam, then whispered, 'I'll tell you what *has* turned up – one of the hedgehogs. Under the great lilac.'

Tom stared, then said, 'No, that's just a patch of moonlight.'

'But it's moving. It's coming towards us.'

There *was* some little creature. 'It can't be a hedgehog,' said Tom, 'unless there are white ones. Could it be a very pale baby rabbit?'

The creature gave a little scurry forward, a sort of miniature gallop, then lay flat on its stomach. And now it was close enough for them to see it clearly.

Pam said, 'It's a kitten! A white kitten! And there's

another coming – out of the cow parsley under the white lilac. And there's another – and another! The orchard's seething with kittens.'

'Keep dead quiet,' whispered Tom.

A black kitten had now caught up with the white kitten, who batted it playfully with a slender paw. Then they rolled over and over together, in a muddle of black and white. A third kitten, a ginger, joined them. And then came the smallest kitten of all. At first they thought it was another white one; then they saw that it had tabby markings, mainly pale grey. The four kittens played together for a few moments, then began moving forward again, sometimes creeping, sometimes leaping, sometimes retreating in sudden alarm; then stealthily moving forward again.

'It's like a kittens' ballet,' whispered Pam.

Tom put his finger on his lips.

Now the kittens were only a few yards from the bread and milk. They stopped, stared at it; then the smallest kitten backed away. The others crept closer, reached the edge of the dish, leaned over it. Then the smallest kitten joined them. Soon the twins could hear the sounds of four tiny tongues lapping.

Slowly the level of the milk in the dish got lower.

Then the kittens started on the bread, doubtfully at first, then gulping it eagerly. But they didn't finish it. The smallest stopped eating first, then the ginger, then the black. The white kitten, which was the largest, went on longest but eventually had enough. They moved a few feet away, then sat down and began to wash themselves, not very expertly; their paws kept slipping.

'Shall we go down and pet them?' said Pam.

'We should scare them. Oh, dear!'

The kittens were dashing away. Within seconds they had vanished into the cow parsley under the great white lilac.

'Was it our voices?' said Pam.

Tom said, 'No. *That's* what it was.'

A few feet from the bread and milk dish were two large hedgehogs.

'They've come for their food,' said Pam. 'Poor hedgehogs!'

'We've still got plenty of milk and the kittens left quite a bit of bread. We'll go down.'

Pam looked along the passage. 'Gram's light's out. We must be careful not to wake her.'

They crept down the stairs and into the sitting room, then looked through the french window. The hedgehogs were still there. Tom opened the window very quietly. The hedgehogs stayed put. The twins dodged out of sight for a few seconds. When they looked out again, the hedgehogs were gone.

'Gram said they'd do that,' said Tom. 'But they may come back.' He poured the rest of the milk into the dish.

'Did you see their little faces? They were even more witchy than I expected. Goodness, how lucky we are! Hedgehogs *and* kittens! We must ask Gram to put out *two* dishes of bread and milk tomorrow.'

Tom bolted the french window, then said, 'Pam, I'm not quite sure we *should* tell Gram about the kittens. Not just suddenly, that is.'

'Why ever not?'

'Well, four kittens is a lot to spring on her. And she's always said she wouldn't replace Mogg.'

'Oh, she'll feel differently once she sees those kittens.'

'Of course she will,' said Tom, heartily. But the heartiness wasn't genuine. He had, for the first time in his life, decided to spare Pam anxiety by not sharing his thoughts with her. It was quite a mature decision and made him feel a little lonely.

'Let's get to bed now,' said Pam. 'Then tomorrow will come quicker.'

3. THE TIGER AND THE SNAKE

Tom woke at seven. The day was already brilliant. He got up and looked out of his window. Across the fields was Freke Hall, the only house to be seen from any window at Himbers. In winter it could be clearly seen, but now that the trees were in full leaf he could only get a glimpse of the roof and chimneys. He was glad they were to see inside that afternoon; it was something to look forward to. But it did not stop him from feeling anxious.

He put on his dressing gown and opened his bedroom door. There was no sound from Pam's room and none from Gram's. He tiptoed along the passage, downstairs and into the sitting room, then unbolted the french window and went out into the orchard.

Mogg's dish was empty and very dirty. The hedgehogs had obviously had their earthy feet in it; Tom could see their claw marks. He went in search of the kittens.

He wondered if their mother would be with them. He found it hard to believe that she would already have left them on their own. Recently he had learned quite a lot about the behaviour of mother cats to their kittens. There had been two fairly large kittens outside the kitchen at school; Cook, with whom he was rather a favourite, had shown them to him. She had told him their mother was a cat living wild and quite untamable.

'If ever you see her, never try to pat her,' said Cook. 'She'll claw you badly. But when she's got kittens she'll come to the back door and take any scraps I put down for her, though what she needs most is milk. After a few weeks she'll bring her kittens with her and show them how to lap and then how to wash themselves – they're ever so quick to copy her. Then a week or so later she'll go off and leave them flat. Once I didn't see her for nearly a year.'

'But what happens to the kittens?' asked Tom.

'Oh, I go on feeding them but fairly soon they

go off, too. I suppose they just live wild, on birds and mice.'

'Birds?' said Tom, in horror. He loved birds. He loved mice too, though he did know you couldn't let a house become overrun with them. 'But couldn't you make pets of the kittens?'

Cook said she'd never managed to stroke them. 'Some say you can never tame a kitten born in the wild. And anyway, I'm thankful when they go. I couldn't keep a lot of cats. But it's sad to think of them fending for themselves when they're still so little.'

Cook asked him not to mention them to anyone, not even Pam, as she didn't want her kitchen invaded by children hoping to see them. Tom went on making daily enquiries until he heard they were gone.

And now were those four exquisite kittens seen by moonlight doomed to face life in the wild? Not yet, surely; they were too young. But something must be done quickly, all the more so as kittens born in the wild were hard to tame; he was not going to believe it was impossible. He and Pam could not do the job in the few days of their half-term holiday. And, anyway, the kittens' future depended on Gram. Could she be enticed into keeping them?

He searched the orchard very thoroughly in the

bright morning sunlight. Blackbirds, thrushes and innumerable sparrows hopped about, taking very little notice of him. How soon would they be in danger from the kittens? Hundreds of birds might have to die to keep the kittens from starvation unless Gram would adopt them.

He went to the edge of the pond by the stepping stones and sat there, looking at the cheerful ducks. Surely they were too large to be in danger – unless all four kittens ganged up on one duck. Dreadful thought. But there was an even worse one, deep in his mind. It had arrived there last night, when Pam had spoken of telling Gram about the kittens. He had remembered that Cook had said that the vet who visited the school pets had told her the kindest thing to do with wild cats and kittens was to catch them and have them painlessly put to sleep, otherwise they lived wretched lives and often ended by dying of starvation. Would Gram feel it was her duty – No, no, no. Gram would find some way out. But she mustn't be *rushed* at.

He sprang up. Suppose Pam had told her already? He'd been in the orchard quite a long time. He turned to go indoors and saw Pam coming through the french window. She called, 'Gram says will you hurry up with your bath? I've had mine. She's getting breakfast.'

He ran as fast as he could. 'Pam, you haven't told her yet – about the kittens?'

'No, I've only seen her for a minute. We'll tell her together, at breakfast.'

He said urgently, 'Will you leave it to me, please? I want to . . . sort of feel my way.'

Pam looked at him quickly. 'You're worried, aren't you? There's no need. Nothing will go wrong about those kittens.'

'You can't be *sure.*'

'I can – but I won't tell you why. You probably wouldn't believe me. Anyway, I'll leave it to you to tell Gram and if you decide to wait a bit I'll follow your lead.'

'Bless you. That's a new shirt.'

It was pale green, with a pattern of daisies.

'Yes, I found it hanging in my cupboard. And there's something new in your chest of drawers. I looked. Now hurry up.'

His spirits rose. He dashed upstairs, started his bath, then ran to his bedroom. There was a new pullover, in a very good shade of blue. Wonderful Gram. *Of course* they could count on her.

When he came downstairs a delightful smell of frying bacon floated towards him. He went through to the kitchen. Gram was at the stove, Pam was manning the electric toaster. The long scrubbed pine table was laid with white pottery on which were the figures of continental peasants, in bright colours. Gram had had this pottery since she was first married and much of it had been broken. The twins especially liked it so she saved what was left for their holiday breakfasts.

Gram was now frying eggs.

'What a breakfast,' said Tom. 'Cook at school says bacon's like gold now.'

'Only bacon's much nicer,' said Pam. 'I shouldn't like a slice of gold for breakfast.' The toaster pinged and she shot up two pieces. She was always pleased if she could make them shoot up high.

'Where's Hildy?' asked Tom.

'Out working on his vegetables,' said Gram. 'He's had his breakfast already.'

'Later I'll go and help him,' said Tom.

'Well, I'm sure he'll value your company. He's a bit independent about being helped.'

'And I shall help you,' said Pam.

'I shall value both your company and your help.

And then we'll have our morning milk and biscuits under the great lilac.'

'Beside it,' said Tom. 'You can't see the bloom if you sit under it.'

Gram brought the big dish of bacon and eggs to the table and served them.

'Goodness, I can't eat all this,' said Pam.

'Try,' said Gram.

Tom, cutting up his bacon, saw a way of leading the conversation to kittens. He said, 'Do you remember how fond of bacon Mogg was, Gram? Do you still miss her?'

'Not as she was in the end. I was always wondering if it was kind to go on keeping her. So I was thankful when she died peacefully in her sleep. But I do miss her as she was when young. Dear Mogg.'

Tom, trying to sound casual, said, 'You don't think a few kittens would comfort you?'

Gram laughed. 'A few? Do you want me to start a cats' home?' But his pretence of casualness had not been lost on her and she went on, anxiously, 'Darling, you're not feeling pet-starved, are you? There are quite a few reasons why we oughtn't to have any, yet. For one thing, you'd hate leaving them when you went back to school and when we went for summer holidays. And this year I want to take you abroad.' And quite time, too, she told herself. She mustn't let the memory of their parents' deaths put her off letting them see something of Europe. 'Though it may be too expensive. Things get worse and worse. Incidentally, it costs a lot to keep pets. You'd be surprised what Mogg cost, for food and vet's bills.'

Pam said, 'Poor Gram! Are you still terribly inflated?'

'You make it sound as if I had indigestion. It's not me that's inflated, it's the state of the world.'

Hildy came in through the open back door, carrying a basket of string beans. He was a slender, thin-faced old man, looking more like a barrister or civil servant, Gram always thought, than a gardener. The twins greeted him affectionately. As usual he said, 'How's school?' and as usual they said, 'Not bad at all.' Then Tom said, 'But it's nicer here. The garden's looking lovely.' And Pam said, 'We could see that, even by moonlight.'

Hildy looked pleased but shook his head. 'Not what I'd like it to be. Not enough rain.' Often he said, 'Too much rain,' or 'Not enough sun.' No weather was ever perfect for his garden.

Hopeless to talk about the kittens now, thought Tom. Still, he'd made a start.

After breakfast he went out with Hildy; Pam helped with household tasks. Then Gram began preparations for lunch. But soon it was time to take a tray of milk and biscuits out to the orchard. There was some old white furniture near the great white lilac and a hammock. Pam was particularly fond of the hammock but she insisted that Gram should take it. Tom joined them but said Hildy wouldn't come. 'He doesn't hold with eating between meals.'

'Neither do I, for grown-ups,' said Gram. 'Though milk's said to be good for old bones.'

'You don't have old bones,' said Tom. 'People with old bones sit down very carefully.'

Pam said, 'I wonder how many heads of lilac there are on that tree. There must be thousands.'

Tom ran his eye over the tree. 'Not thousands, but there are a good many hundred. Let's count. You do this half. I'll do the other.'

Gram, lying back in her hammock, thought, *Another memory of that tree to store up*. She could remember her husband, not long after the tree was planted, proudly counting twenty heads of blossom.

Soon Pam said, 'It's very difficult. The heads

somehow blur into each other. But I've counted over two hundred.'

'I've counted over three hundred,' said Tom, 'but I'm sure there are more. There might even be a thousand on the whole tree.'

'It's a very important year for that tree,' said Pam. But when Tom asked her why, she just said, 'Oh, I happen to know it is,' and went back to her milk.

Gram said, 'Your grandfather and I planted plenty of lilacs the year we first came here and they've all done quite well. But none of them are like that tree. You should make up a story about it, Pam. It's a long time since you told me one of your stories. Do you remember the tiger in the wood?'

'I think that cured me of making up stories,' said Pam.

'I never wanted to do that. I just wanted to cure you of saying they were true when they weren't. You really frightened me about your tiger,' Gram laughed, remembering.

It had happened last summer. Pam, taking a little walk on her own, had rushed in to say that she had seen a tiger asleep in a nearby wood. She had described it vividly, said how beautiful it had looked with the sunlight filtering through the leaves on to it, how gentle and peaceful. 'At first I thought it must be dead. Then I saw it was breathing, deeply. Its side kept moving in and out.'

There was a private zoo some fifteen miles away. Gram had called Tom and Hildy in from the garden, told them to bolt the front and back doors, and herself bolted the french window. Now, whom should she telephone first, the owner of the zoo or the police? The police, surely; they could set about warning people. Should she ring the local police or dial 999? She dashed to the telephone. Pam, bewildered by her grandmother's whirl of activity, only now realised what had happened. She cried, 'Stop, Gram, please stop! It's only a pretend tiger.'

Gram was too relieved to be angry – and, anyway, she felt she had no right to be angry. Since babyhood Pam had occasionally told most vivid pretend stories, but they had always been about fairies, witches, animals that talked . . . obviously invented. Gram had liked them, often asked for details, marvelling at Pam's imagination. But never had there been a pretend story that could be true – and Gram had, very recently, seen an escaped wolf on television. Gently, and with them all laughing a lot, she had explained that now Pam was nine and went to school, and was normally particularly truthful, she really ought not to invent stories which might be accepted as true. She had added, 'Not that I want to curb your imagination. I love your stories. But you should just give me a little hint that they're not true. Even a wink would do.'

Pam had said she would be most careful in future, but she soon found that she had no desire to tell pretend stories if they were, from the outset, admittedly pretend stories. They had, in some strange way, seemed real to her. They never would again.

She said now, 'I never told you another pretend story.'

Gram smiled. 'Well, there was just the snake. That fooled me again.'

'Ah, yes, the snake,' said Pam. 'I'd forgotten that.' But she hadn't and she was quite sure she never would – and now it had caused her to tell another lie. For she had only said it was a pretend story to save the snake's life.

It had happened not very long after the tiger story. She had seen the most beautiful snake curled up at the far end of the orchard. She had gazed at it lovingly, then tiptoed away and dashed indoors to tell anyone she could find, to share the snake with them, to bring them back to admire it. But as soon as she had described it Gram had looked worried and Hildy had said, 'I'll get a stick – no, a spade would be best,' Pam had screamed, 'No, no, it's a *good* snake. I recognised it.'

Tom had said, 'We had a lesson on snakes at school. It's very likely to be harmless.'

But in Hildy's view, no snake should be accepted as harmless when there were children around. He had marched purposefully to the door. Pam had flung herself at her grandmother, shrieking, 'Please, please don't let him! I'm terribly sorry but it's just a pretend snake.'

Gram had looked annoyed; then said, 'Well, you did own up quickly.'

It was the first out-and-out lie Pam had ever told. She had felt so guilty that she never even told Tom about it. And now she had told another lie, saying she had forgotten the snake. But she still did not feel truly repentant. She decided she would rather have two lies on her conscience than that the snake should have had its beautiful head chopped off. Where was it now? She imagined it coming to meet her one day, to thank her.

When they had finished their milk and biscuits

Gram went back to the kitchen, having declined Pam's help. 'You two have done enough for one morning. Just enjoy yourselves.'

Pam got into the hammock and asked Tom to swing her. He obliged but his mind wasn't on it. Quite soon he said, 'Well, I didn't make a good start about the kittens at breakfast. Do you really think things will be all right for them?'

'I do.' Pam closed her eyes and looked blissful.

'I wish you'd tell me why.'

'Perhaps I will, after we see them tonight.'

'I shan't tell Gram unless they come again. They may not.'

'They will.' Pam opened her eyes and looked up at the lilac tree. 'They'll suddenly be here, under this tree. Go on swinging me.'

'Hammocks aren't really meant to swing in. And we've a perfectly good swing where you can swing yourself.'

'Yes, but you can't lie down for it.' She closed her eyes again.

Tom, gently pushing the hammock, looked at her peaceful face and thought how little he knew about what was going on in her mind. Some twins, he believed, often knew what each other was thinking but he never did, with Pam. Sometimes, through knowing her very well, he could make a *guess* but he never knew for certain. And now she might well have been on another planet for all he knew of her thoughts. How could she possibly know what would happen about the kittens?

After a while he said, 'There is nothing more boring than pushing a person in a hammock – unless it's being expected to tickle their arms.'

'Oh, that's lovely,' said Pam. 'Especially when it's done with a feathery piece of grass.'

'Well, it's not going to be done,' said Tom. 'I'm going for a walk.'

Pam opened her eyes again and said politely, 'Anyway, thank you for swinging me.' She then returned to her thoughts – which were not, at the moment, concerned with Tom. It had never occurred to her to wonder what was going on in his mind, but she quite often knew it, and accepted this as perfectly normal.

At one o'clock Gram rang a bell for lunch in the kitchen. When the twins got in, Hildy was helping with the dishing up. Although he enjoyed having meals with the family, he still considered it a privilege, rather than the normal thing, and was eager to wait on everyone. The twins were equally eager to wait on him. Today, Tom pushed him firmly into his chair and said, 'Hildy, please stay put and give your legs a rest.'

There was roast lamb. Pam regarded it with pleasure and then with distress. She said, 'I do love lamb, but I love lambs, too. I suppose one ought to be a vegetarian.'

'There are some at school,' said Tom, 'but it doesn't really count because they eat animal products, milk, cheese, butter, etc. And you can't keep cows only for their milk; if you did, you'd have to kill off the bull calves. Mike says the only logical vegetarians are vegans, who eat no animal produce at all. Mike admires but he won't accept them; he says they're too difficult to feed. And he points out that if all the world became vegans, cows, pigs and sheep, etc, would have no life at all, except for a few in zoos or animal reserves.'

Hildy said, 'Well, those that never got born wouldn't know what they'd missed, and they would be saved from suffering.'

'The same applies to *us*,' said Tom. 'Mike says that if the whole human race was wiped out, we'd be saved a powerful lot of suffering, but none of us would choose not to have been born. Mike thinks it's better to have lived and died than never to have lived at all. Anyway, Mike says the animals are better off than we are, in one way – they don't know death's ahead of them. We do.'

'*I* don't,' said Pam. 'I simply don't believe in it. And if everyone felt as I do, it would stop happening. I think everyone and everything – every human being, animal, tree, even every blade of grass – should live for ever.'

'But there wouldn't be room for them,' said her brother.

'God ought to be able to arrange it, if all things are possible to him. But just look at what he's let happen, for millions and millions of years – all the death and misery and horror. Really, the kindest thing one can do for God is not to believe in him.'

'Which reminds me,' said Gram. 'Our dear vicar's dear wife will be taking the entrance money at Freke Hall this afternoon. I'd be obliged if you didn't mention your atheism to her.'

'Oh, I'll lay off it,' said Pam. 'I'm not a militant atheist. But do I have to go to church tomorrow?'

'No, I've found a way out of that. We're going to drive into Norfolk and have lunch on the way. I want to visit an old friend in a nursing home.'

'*What* old friend?' said Tom. 'I seem to remember . . .'

'Yes, it *is* Miss Jellicoe. But you won't have to see her.'

'I should hope not,' said Tom. 'And I shouldn't think she'd want us to, seeing that the last time we saw her she said rude things about us even before we were out of the room.'

'Well, you were *just* out; unfortunately she has a very carrying voice. Anyway, the nursing home she's gone to has beautiful grounds; you'll enjoy seeing those. And we'll have lunch at an old coaching inn.'

'I bet it won't be a better lunch than this one,' said Pam. She turned her eyes to a large saucepan bubbling on the stove. 'Would that be a syrup treacle roly-poly?'

'I know how much both of you like that,' said Gram.

Tom said, 'Mike says all modern children prefer ice cream to what he calls heavy puddings. But he's wrong.'

'Why not tell him?' said Hildy.

'Well, it might hurt his feelings. And ice cream does save a lot of cooking. Anyway, we like looking forward to Gram's puddings.'

Gram basked. Much as she liked and admired the twins' headmaster, there were times when she heard the phrase 'Mike says' rather too often. She found it pleasant, while unpinning the roly-poly from its pudding cloth, to feel she was one up on Mike.

4. FREKE HALL

After lunch they all got ready to go to Freke Hall, except Hildy, who said he'd rather watch sport on television.

'Well, mind you do,' said Gram. 'Don't keep getting up to do some odd jobs. You're not supposed to work on Saturday afternoons.'

He gave a non-committal 'Hmm' and went to bring the car round.

'Couldn't we just walk across the fields?' said Tom.

'We'd have to cross the old railway line,' said Gram. 'The banks are overgrown now and there's a lot of barbed wire. Which reminds me, I don't want you two walking along the tracks any more. It's too secluded – except at weekends, and then there are a lot of courting couples.'

'We don't mind courting couples,' said Pam.

'It's tactful to leave courting couples on their own,' said Gram.

They went out, ready for Hildy with the car. He said he'd have tea waiting for them.

'Will you drive through the village rather fast, Gram?' said Tom, 'in case someone stops you?'

'Why should anyone stop me?'

'Well, they do if we walk in the village with you. And after they've said "How's school?" and not given us time to answer, they tell you someone's ill, or ask what you thought of the last cheese and wine party and if you're coming to the next one.'

Gram laughed. 'I must say there have been a spate of cheese and wine parties, but they do bring in money for various good causes. As for illness, there always *is* someone ill in a village. There must be far more ill people in towns, of course, but people in towns seldom know their neighbours.'

The village was pretty but not at its best at the weekends as too many people came to admire its prettiness. Gram said, 'When your grandfather and I first came here there was only one shop and no café. Now there are ten shops and three cafés, not to mention four pubs. Well, one should be willing to share with the poor, jaded townsfolk, but I'm thankful I live two miles away.'

The church clock chimed three.

Pam said, 'As an atheist, I find churches worrying. I want them to last for ever – anyway, I want the old ones to. But I've no right to expect other people to keep them alive.'

'Perhaps they'll end up as ruins, like so many castles,' said Tom.

Gram said, 'Ruined castles are beautiful but I once saw a ruined church and it was depressing. And I once saw a beautiful old church being pulled down and I felt it was outrageous.'

'Pulled down? A consecrated church? That seems to me shocking,' said Pam.

'I'd say your atheism's quite a bit shaky,' said her brother.

They took a narrow road out of the village which at first led through cultivated land and then through a neglected stretch of countryside. There were some tangled woods, water meadows running down to a stream, and then traces of a hamlet where a few cottages were still standing but none of them fit to occupy. They had once belonged to the departed Freke family.

'It's a shame they've just been allowed to fall down,' said Gram. 'I'm afraid they've all gone too far to be saved now. Well, there's the Hall.'

The tall wrought iron gates were open. A winding drive led through a thick shrubbery which hid the ground floor of the house from them. When it came in sight the twins gasped in dismay.

'They've cut down all the bushes,' said Pam. 'And torn down the creepers.'

'Well, I told you they've been tidying up,' said Gram. 'I must say it looks bare now but I understand it's a start towards restoring the gardens. We'll just have to be patient.'

They parked the car and got out. The heavy oak door was open and the vicar's wife was seated at a table indoors. She greeted them by saying, 'Well, I'm glad someone's turned up,' smiled at the twins and said, 'How's school?' then turned to their grandmother. 'Have you heard about poor Mary Hallam? Both her parents are ill.'

Gram said hastily, 'Run and look round the gardens, darlings, while I get our tickets.'

The twins managed to get out of earshot before they laughed. Then Tom said, 'Well, she didn't get as far as cheese and wine parties.'

'She will,' said Pam. She gazed around. 'Oh, dear! How awful it is now! The poor shorn bushes look like giant stubble.'

'Perhaps in a few years this'll be velvet lawns and rose gardens,' said Tom.

'And customers buying garden furniture. Perhaps they'll have tea under coloured umbrellas.' Pam then rebuked herself. 'Mike would tell us not to be sneery. The great thing is that the house will be saved.'

They were at the back now. A diamond-paned window stood open. They looked in through it.

'There's a pump, right in the middle of the kitchen,' said Pam. 'Fascinating.'

'Let's go back and see if Gram's finished talking.'

'You mean listening.'

She hadn't and they guessed she was quite relieved to stop. She said to the vicar's wife, 'Well, let me know if I can help,' then led the twins into the house.

'How are poor Mary Hallam's parents?' whispered Tom.

'In a bad way, I fear, but there's no need for you to worry about it. Now let's see. This must be the Great Hall.'

There was a fine window reaching almost to the high ceiling, but some of its sections had been boarded up and much of the remaining glass was cracked. The twins, who had visited several great houses open to the public, were looking round critically.

'The fireplace has been spoilt,' said Tom. 'And the panelling isn't real. It's a sort of embossed wallpaper.'

'I believe it's some stuff that used to be called Lincrusta,' said Gram. 'Perhaps they used it because the panelling had gone.'

'It would improve things if you whitewashed the walls,' said Pam, 'and there may be the original fireplace behind that tiled one.'

Gram opened a door into a large room with faded floral wallpaper. 'This was probably the drawing room.'

'What on earth are those?' said Tom.

On either side of another tiled fireplace were white-painted structures rather like summer houses without roofs. Inside them were numerous shelves and little mirrors, and padded velvet seats, now faded.

Gram said, 'They're Edwardian cosy-corners. There was one in my grandmother's house. They could look quite pretty with lots of ornaments in them. But I suppose you think they're funny.'

But the twins liked them. Tom said that by now they were almost antiques. And Pam said she'd keep them, if it were her house, and also the fireplace, where the tiles had roses on them. 'I'd make the whole room Edwardian. It's quite an interesting period.'

Gram, born half a century before the twins, had always thought of the Edwardian period as merely old-fashioned. She now decided to treat it with more respect – and wondered how much interesting Edwardiana she had, during her lifetime, got rid of.

They went back to the hall and then into the dining room where the only object of interest was a built-in mahogany sideboard.

'Dull but worthy,' pronounced Tom.

'Nothing whatever in the drawers,' said Pam. 'I wish they hadn't cleaned the house so thoroughly. Well, I've hopes of the kitchen.'

They found it at the end of a long passage. 'What a distance to carry the food,' said Gram.

Tom, looking around him eagerly, said, 'This really is something.'

There was a vast stone sink, a vast iron kitchen range, two enormous dressers, a long row of iron bells and, most interesting of all, the pump.

'It must connect with a well,' said Gram. 'I suppose it's under the kitchen.'

'I wonder if it still works,' said Tom, pumping. A trickle of water came out.

Gram stopped him hastily. 'You'll flood the kitchen.'

'Is there mains water now?' asked Pam.

'No, indeed, nor electricity. They'll have to bring them from quite a long way off.'

There were various rooms leading off the kitchen, a larder, two store rooms and a large room Gram thought must have been the Servants' Hall. 'When we first came here there was an old lady alive in the village who remembered visiting the Freke family. She said there must have been at least ten servants.'

'How strange to think of them all here,' said Pam. 'I like this part of the house. It feels real.'

'Presumably the servants didn't get the benefit of Edwardian improvements,' said Gram. 'I find it hard to believe that seventy years ago they put up with this kitchen.'

There was a back staircase, dark and narrow. Pam, leading the way, said, 'Just think of the maids carrying cans of hot water up. I don't suppose there'll be a bathroom.'

But they found one, on the first floor, with a huge, cracked bath and brass taps green with verdigris.

'And as there's HOT on one of them, there must be some kind of hot water system,' said Gram. 'I must say that's a striking loo. It's art nouveau. That would have been the latest thing in the early 1900s.'

They tramped through a number of dull bedrooms, some with art nouveau wallpapers. 'I know it's fashionable again,' said Gram, 'but I still dislike it. How *could* anyone so spoil a beautiful Tudor house?'

Then Tom opened a heavy door and cried, 'Come on – quickly. At last there's a wonderful room.'

It ran the full depth of the house and almost all of it was panelled. There were four deep window embrasures and much of the glass was old and in fair condition. And at each end of the room was an unspoilt open fireplace.

'It's what's called a Long Gallery,' said Tom. 'I believe ladies used to take exercise in them when the weather was bad.'

'Oh, I've just remembered,' said Gram. 'The old lady I told you about described this Gallery to me and she said there was supposed to be a secret room in it.'

'Where?' said both the twins together.

'She didn't say. She only said there was supposed to be one.'

'We must find it,' said Tom. 'We must knock on all the panels until we hear a hollow sound.'

'I don't quite know how a hollow sound would sound,' said Pam.

'Well, it would sound empty,' said Tom. 'Come on.'

They walked round, knocking and listening.

'You're making rather a lot of noise,' said Gram.

'It's terribly important,' said Tom. 'We've always wanted to find a secret room.'

So had Gram, as a child, and she found she would still like to. She joined in the knocking and listening.

After a few minutes the vicar's wife came hurrying in and was relieved to see them. She said she had feared they were shut in somewhere and were knocking for help. Told about the possibility of a secret room she said she, too, had longed to find one and would join in the hunt. There was now so much knocking that it was difficult to listen – 'Especially when you're listening for a sound that isn't there,' said Pam.

They gave up and Tom suggested they should now explore the attics, but the vicar's wife said the door to them had been locked. 'Some of the floors are rotten and there's nothing to be seen. They're not much more than garrets.'

'Garrets might be fascinating,' said Pam.

'I don't suppose the servants thought they were,' said Gram.

They went down to the Great Hall by a wide staircase. Tom, eyeing it expertly, said he didn't think it was the original one.

Gram thought that only the Long Gallery had been worth seeing but the twins had liked the kitchen. 'And those cosy-corners were rather pets,' said Pam.

The vicar's wife went back to her table, saying she supposed she must stay until six though she doubted if anyone else would come. 'And then I shall lock the door for the last time and on Monday the builders and decorators will take over.'

'Well, they can't make it much worse,' said Tom. 'And it may end up *looking* better, even if it is mainly fake antiquity.'

They went out into the bright afternoon. Pam said, 'We'll come back in the summer holidays and see how they're getting on.'

But they were fated to come back to Freke Hall long before that.

5. THE SECOND MIDNIGHT

Hildy had a splendid tea waiting for them and then there was good television; they watched it almost all evening and had supper on trays. Around ten o'clock Gram hinted it might be time to go to bed but didn't press it.

The twins had decided to stay up as late as possible because Pam was convinced that the kittens would not turn up until midnight. And if the food was put out too early, the hedgehogs might take it all.

'In that case we'd put out some more,' said Tom. 'And you can't possibly be sure they won't come till midnight.' Still, he agreed it was best to stay up late, so that Gram would be safely in bed before he and Pam began watching the orchard.

At eleven o'clock he asked if he should get the

bread and milk for the hedgehogs. 'And can I give them two dishes tonight, Gram, as they seemed so hungry?'

Gram told him to take as much as he liked and also to take some milk and cake for himself and Pam. He found a large, shallow dish and filled both it and Mogg's old dish to overflowing. Gram, coming into the kitchen, said, 'Good heavens, you've got enough for an army of hedgehogs,' but she raised no objection and helped him to carry everything through to the sitting room.

Pam was standing by the open french window. She said, 'No sign of hedgehogs yet,' which Tom took to mean that the orchard was clear of kittens. He put the two dishes out, then came in and bolted the french window. Pam then said she was ready for bed, kissed her grandmother goodnight and whisked herself upstairs, intending to watch her hedgehogs.

'Well, that was a sudden exit,' said Gram. 'I expect she suddenly feels tired. I know I do. Put the kitchen lights off, will you, Tom? And see that the front and back doors are bolted. Goodnight, darling.'

When Tom got back to the sitting room he switched the lights off and looked out at the orchard. The moon was so bright that he could see as far as the lilac tree. Still no kittens. Would he be sorry if they did not come again – or would he be relieved? He simply did not know. He picked up the tray of milk and cake Gram had left and went upstairs.

Pam was already in her dressing gown and sitting on the landing window seat, with the lights off. 'Hurry up,' she said. 'It'll be midnight soon.'

'Not for twenty minutes,' said Tom. Still, he hurried.

Soon after he got back, Pam said, 'Gram's light's just gone off.'

'Lucky she's not the kind of grandmother who feels she has to tuck us up in bed.'

After what seemed like ages but was really only five minutes by Tom's watch, Pam whispered, 'Look, the hedgehogs! Shall we scare them off?'

'No,' said Tom. 'They're entitled to their whack.' Apart from wanting to be fair to hedgehogs, he wanted to watch them.

They were moving slowly, cautiously. When they came to the two dishes each hedgehog took over a dish, plunged its pointed nose in and drank. After a while, one hedgehog put its feet on the edge of its dish and tilted it, to get more milk – which then ran over its nose. The other hedgehog also tried to tilt its dish but hadn't the knack of it, so got right into the dish and went on drinking.

'They're taking everything,' whispered Pam. 'Oughn't we to scare them off now?'

'Not unless they take too much bread. We've plenty of milk to fill up.'

Suddenly both hedgehogs were off, incredibly fast.

'I wonder if they heard us,' said Tom. 'I hope they've had enough.'

'Well, they've had all they're getting now. Quick, take more milk down. It must be nearly midnight.'

Tom got his torch from his dressing-gown pocket to light himself down the stairs to the sitting room. Pam stayed at the landing window, watching. When he got back he said, 'There was plenty of milk left and I've filled the dishes to overflowing.' He looked at his watch. 'It's midnight now, Pam.'

The church clock began to strike.

'Now!' said Pam, gazing out at the lilac tree.

They counted the strokes. By the twelfth stroke there were still no kittens.

'You can't expect them to arrive on the dot,' said Tom.

'I can! I do! They have!'

The kittens were suddenly *there*, on their way from the lilac tree.

'Why didn't we see them coming?' said Tom.

'Because they didn't come, they *appeared*. They're *magic* kittens! Ssh!'

Tonight the four kittens came forward at the same time, the white one and the black one slightly ahead of the other two. They moved stealthily, as if stalking something. Then the black kitten pounced

– on nothing. Then the white kitten appeared to go crazy and ran round and round in wide circles. The ginger kitten and the pale tabby followed it and then ended up by trying to climb a tree. They stood on their hind legs and put their paws up but had not, yet, the strength or skill for climbing. Then they noticed that the black kitten had gone on by itself and reached the bread and milk. They set off after it at full gallop. A few seconds later, all four kittens were grouped round one of the dishes.

Tonight they cleared it of bread as well as milk, then moved away. Then the white kitten saw the second dish and dashed to it. The others followed and they all lapped some more milk but didn't eat more bread. Soon they stopped lapping. They'd had enough.

Their washing tonight was more expert and, as nothing scared them, went on longer. At last they all tucked their front paws under them, closed their eyes, and dozed.

After a few minutes Pam said, 'We'll go down to them. I *know* it'll be all right.'

But that moment a distant owl hooted and all the kittens heard it. They were off instantly, racing into the orchard.

'Watch them! Watch them!' said Tom. 'See where they go.'

But he didn't manage it and Pam didn't even try. She said, 'They don't *go*. They vanish.'

Tom stared at her. 'Do you really believe they're magic?'

'Of course. I knew last night when they appeared at midnight. But I wasn't going to tell you until it had happened again.'

Tom said, 'The fact that they come at midnight is very strange but lots of strange things happen. They can't really be magic or they wouldn't need to eat.'

'Of course they would. What about leprechauns in Ireland? What about the Little People, who help housewives if cakes are put out for them? The magic world and the real world sort of overlap.'

'Well, magic or not magic, they'll have to be fed. And we can't arrange for that after we go back to school on Tuesday. We've got to tell Gram.'

'All right. We'll tell her tomorrow morning. She won't mind. Nothing can go wrong for magic kittens.'

He was suddenly angry. How could Pam, exactly the same age as he was, be so babyish? It wasn't only that she believed in magic. He, himself, though he couldn't share her belief in fairyland magic, could believe in many inexplicable happenings. He remembered Mike quoting from *Hamlet*: 'There are more things in heaven and earth, Horatio, than are dreamt of in your philosophy.' Tom felt he could believe anything that Shakespeare had believed. But why couldn't Pam see that, as Gram didn't want kittens, danger might threaten them?

He closed the window quietly. At least the kittens were full of food for the moment, and it was a fine, warm night for them. Where were they? No use being angry with Pam, and he wasn't exactly angry, it was more a feeling of distress that he and she could be so different.

He said firmly, 'We'll tell Gram first thing tomorrow.'

But when they came down in the morning Gram had already gone out. Hildy, making preparations for breakfast, said she had gone down to the village to see Miss Hallam. 'It's those parents of hers – both ill at the same time. But your gram said you weren't to worry. She'll be back by ten-thirty and will you please be ready to jump into the car? It's a nice day for your drive. Going to see Miss Jellicoe, aren't you?'

'Gram is. She says we needn't,' said Pam. 'Miss

Jellicoe, Miss Hallam – poor Gram always has to help someone.'

'Never could stand Miss Jellicoe,' said Hildy. 'I used to help out with her garden, but she was so rude that your gram wouldn't lend me to her any more. The real reason Miss J's gone into a nursing home is that she can't get people to work for her. She's not ill. Well, it's lucky she's rich.' He started to fry eggs.

Over breakfast Tom considered telling Hildy about the kittens but decided against it. Hildy was not, in general, fond of cats. Even Mogg had been unpopular with him when she scratched in flower beds or clawed the bark of trees.

After breakfast the twins walked round the orchard together. The sun shone, a light breeze swayed the cow parsley, birds sang, ducks quacked – but there were no kittens to be seen.

'Well, of course not,' said Pam. 'They won't appear till midnight. Shall we tell Gram about them during the drive?'

'No. She doesn't like to talk too much when she's driving. And she'll be worried about the Hallams.'

But when Gram came back from the village she seemed quite cheerful and when Tom politely enquired about the Hallams he was told, 'Nothing for you to worry about. I've arranged for someone to give a helping hand all day. So off we go and let's enjoy ourselves.'

And so they did. Gram knew many interesting little roads which avoided main roads and took them through their favourite Suffolk villages. And gradually they got further afield and saw new places. Pam said she loved seeing a place for the first time and Tom said he did, too, but he also liked coming back to a place he knew well. And Gram remembered seeing all these places with her husband, in their early days at Himbers. She didn't mention this in case the twins should think she was sad – which, indeed, she wasn't. It never failed to astonish her that one could get over the loss of someone deeply loved, yet without loving the lost one any less.

They had lunch at a pleasant old coaching inn. It was some years since Gram had been there and she was startled by the prices on the menu. So were the twins. Tom said, 'Gram, this place is ruinous.' And Pam, who had been thinking of stagecoaches and highwaymen, suddenly came down to earth and said, 'It's not fair to you, Gram. Shall we go somewhere else?'

Gram said, 'When you are taken out for a meal you must never look at the prices on the menu – or, if you do look, you must pretend you haven't. It's all due to inflation; the high cost of food and of labour.'

Pam said they would order *à la carte* and only have one thing each. But Gram said one never could stick to that and *à la carte* always ended by costing more. 'We'll have the *table d'hôte* – there's plenty of choice. And now stop talking about the price. It's bad manners when you're my guests.'

What Tom thought was that the cost of their meal would have fed the four kittens for months. But he wasn't going to mention the kittens until they got home and Gram could see them and fall in love with them.

It was, anyway, a very good lunch and if the food wasn't quite as good as what Gram gave them at home, it was fun having it in a hotel.

They reached the nursing home in the early afternoon. It was in very pleasant country and quite unlike what the twins had expected. They had imagined it would resemble the hospital where they had once visited a school friend, but what they saw was just a very large red brick house with a great many windows, balconies and turrets. Gram said it had been built in the very early 1900s and that, though she had thought on her first visit that the architecture was hideous, she had begun to like it. 'And inside it's so pretty and cheerful – it's really more of a home than a nursing home, a sort of hotel for people who need waiting on all the time.'

The hall smelt of lavender wax polish and there were tall, beautifully arranged vases of flowers. A smiling young nurse in a mauve uniform came to meet them and recognised Gram. When the twins were introduced she looked at Gram quickly and said, 'Were you thinking of taking them up? I must warn you, it's not one of her good days.'

'Does she have any?' said Tom.

The nurse laughed. 'I see you know her. Oh, she's not so bad, now we've got used to her. But she *is* hard to please.'

'You're not thinking of turning her out?' said Gram anxiously.

The nurse laughed again. 'Oh, dear me, no! We take quite a pride in coping with her. And we have had worse – though not much. Anyway, she's in excellent health, even better than when she first came here.'

'I must brace myself,' said Gram. 'And you won't

mind if the children explore the gardens. I can take myself up.' She got into the waiting lift.

Tom, who had been looking round the hall with interest, now concentrated on a large board, lettered with the names of people in the nursing home. He said to the nurse, 'I see you have a Miss Freke here. Would she be connected with an old house quite close to where we live called Freke Hall?'

'Yes, she lived there as a child – she often talks about it,' said the nurse, and when she heard that the twins had been inside it she said she wondered if the old lady would like to see them. 'Just wait and I'll find out.' She rang for the lift, then added, 'That is, if you wouldn't mind. She's a very sweet old lady, not a bit like Miss Jellicoe.'

The twins politely said they would be delighted; though after the lift had gone up, Pam said she would have preferred to see the gardens. 'Me, too,' said Tom. 'Still, Miss Freke might tell us something interesting about Freke Hall. She must be very old if she lived there as a child.'

But neither of them was prepared for just how old she was. When the nurse came back and took them up in the lift she said, 'Dear Miss Freke is our very oldest inhabitant. Tomorrow she will be a hundred.'

The twins both said, 'How wonderful!' and Tom really felt it would be wonderful to see such an old lady. Pam was suddenly nervous. She had seen very old people on television and sometimes found them very ugly. Suppose she looked at Miss Freke in horror and hurt her feelings. She mustn't, she mustn't, not for one single second.

Once out of the lift, the nurse took them along a wide passage, saying, 'I'll just show you in and then I must hurry back to the hall.' She opened a door, said, 'Here are the children, Miss Freke,' and went, closing the door behind her.

6. MISS FREKE

The room had one very large window and a small, semi-circular window in a turret. Everything was light and airy. Outside, the summer sky was palest blue. Inside, the walls were palest green, and on them were a great many little pictures of landscapes, children, animals. Above these were shelves on which were delicate china figures. There were several flowering plants, a large bowl of roses, a gilded birdcage in which a canary sang. Everywhere the twins looked there was something pretty.

Pam gave a little gasp and murmured, 'What a lovely room!'

A high, sweet voice said, 'I'm so glad you like it. I always hope it will make up for the fact that the person who lives in it isn't lovely at all.'

The twins turned quickly to the bed, which had a lace bedspread and lace-covered pillows. Above it was a silver crown from which descended green chiffon draperies. And amid the lace and chiffon was a tiny woman wearing a lace bed-jacket, a small muslin ruff and a lace bonnet with a high, pleated frill. Between the frill and the ruff was a small, pointed face with large, dark, sunken eyes. It did not look as big as a normal face; both of the twins thought it could have been a doll's head that leaned back against the lacy pillows. The doll came to life and held out tiny hands in white silk mittens.

'Come and sit beside me, dear children,' said Miss Freke. 'You may sit on the bed. Nurses don't like visitors to sit on beds but they let my visitors do just what I like. You see, I'm very spoilt. They seem to think it clever of me to live to be so old. You're staring at me very strangely. Do I frighten you?'

'Goodness, no,' said Tom. And Pam said, 'It's because you're like someone in a fairy tale.'

Miss Freke looked pleased. 'That's just my trimmings. When I first came here, twenty years ago, I said, "Everything shall be pretty. And the walls shall be my art gallery." I have different pictures for different seasons and I'm always sending for new ones. And I can see them all. There was a time when I thought I was losing my sight, but I worked very hard at my eye exercises and it all came back. And I'm not at all deaf. My doctor tells me I'm freak by nature as well as Freke by name. Still, I think he's quite proud of me. But sometimes I tire, quite suddenly, so please tell me all about Freke Hall while I'm still fresh. I know what's been happening to it – there was something in a local paper. I'm so glad it's going to be used at last.'

The twins began describing their visit, but felt hampered because they hadn't liked most of the house. Pam said, 'Our grandmother thinks much of it was altered in the Edwardian period.'

'That's long after my time,' said Miss Freke. 'It's ninety years since I lived there. We children didn't see much of the downstairs rooms. I dimly remember they were full of heavy furniture and dark draperies. Our special room was called the Long Gallery. It was thought to be old-fashioned so we were

allowed to use it as a playroom. There was a nursery in the attics but it was very dark and horrid. The Long Gallery was marvellous for games. Has it been spoilt now?'

'No!' said the twins eagerly and told her about the panelling, the beautiful windows, the two fireplaces. She kept interrupting with her own memories and they soon realised she was more interested in talking than in listening. Gradually they gathered how she had been connected with Freke Hall. Her father, a younger son, had been in the Indian Army and she had been sent home to live with his elder brother and her young cousins. And then, when she was ten years old, there had been what she described as 'family troubles' and she had been sent to a boarding school; and later she had rejoined her parents and lived in India and other places. The twins found her a little difficult to follow as she was covering nearly a hundred years of her life, jumping from place to place and going backwards and forwards in time, all in her tiny, twittering voice and talking at breakneck speed.

At last she interrupted herself and said, 'Oh, my dear, dear children, how much too much I talk and how much too fast.'

She lay back against her pillows with her eyes closed. But quite soon she opened them again and said, 'No, I'm not tired yet. Tell me some more about the Long Gallery. I did so love it, especially the secret room, which was my own special secret.'

'You mean there really is one?' said Pam.

'Oh, tell us, please,' said Tom. 'Tell us how to find it.'

Miss Freke closed her eyes again, then opened them, saying, 'Yes, yes, I remember perfectly. You stand facing the fireplace at the back of the house. Then look at the panels on your left. Count three panels up and four to the left. You'll then find a panel with three knots in the wood. Press the highest knot *hard*. It should release a spring and then a section of the panelling should open.'

'If only we'd known about this yesterday,' said Tom.

'There's a little room, no larger than a cupboard,' said Miss Freke, and now she was absorbed in her memories again. 'I found it when I was all on my own and never let my cousins know. And on my last day in the house, I hid something there, a great treasure, a little picture. But I can't remember what it was a picture of.' She shook her head sadly. 'My memory's not what it was.'

Tom said, 'I think your memory's marvellous. Fancy remembering how to find the secret room, after all these years. "Three panels up and four to the left. Then press the highest knot of three." Is that what you said?'

'Is it?' Miss Freke's dark eyes now looked vague. 'It's strange how I sometimes remember things in a flash – and then they're gone. Now let me think.' She closed her eyes again.

The door opened and the nurse came in and said, 'Are you getting tired, Miss Freke? Anyway, the children's grandmother's waiting for them now.'

'Oh, dear!' said Miss Freke. 'We're so much enjoying ourselves. Still, I do have to be careful because of tomorrow.' She explained to the twins. 'I'm to be interviewed for television because it's my hundredth birthday. I don't much want to be on television, but I'd like people to see my pretty room. And there won't be much of me to be seen, only the bit of face between my ruff and my bonnet and just the tips of my fingers.' She waved her mittened hands. 'The television people are coming in the morning. And then, in the afternoon, I'm having a tea party here for my nurses, there'll be a cake with a hundred candles. Oh, I wonder –' She was suddenly alive with eagerness. 'I wonder if your grandmother could bring you to my party? Could that be managed, nurse?'

The nurse said she would see, then told the twins to say goodbye. Miss Freke gave a tiny hand to each of them and smiled very sweetly.

Tom said, 'We have been honoured to know you.' And Pam said how much they hoped they could come to the party.

'Do,' said Miss Freke. 'And be sure to get here by four. Then you can help me to blow all those candles out.'

On the way down in the lift the nurse said, 'We must do our best to coax your grandmother. We try never to disappoint Miss Freke.'

Gram didn't need any coaxing for she saw at once how eager the twins were; and she, herself, would be interested to meet Miss Freke. Still, it was a long journey to make, two days running. Now she wasn't looking forward to the drive home as she would have to drive faster than she cared to. Mary Hallam was almost certain to telephone. If only Mary had some of Miss Jellicoe's money and could afford to put her parents into this charming place! Not that Miss Jellicoe found it charming. Gram was glad to forget her and listen to the twins' excited chatter about Miss Freke; though in the end she had to ask them not to talk, so that she could concentrate on driving.

None of them enjoyed the journey. Gram kept telling herself that safety was far more important than getting back quickly, but she never relaxed. The twins felt worried for her, especially as there was quite a lot of traffic. Gram said that was probably due to people going out to have Sunday supper with each other.

When they got home at last they found a note from Hildy. Miss Hallam had telephoned and she, too, was now ill; or rather, she had sprained her back. Hildy was just off to the village on his bicycle to see what odd jobs he could do to help.

Gram said she must go at once and would the twins get themselves some supper; she'd meant to give them tea on the way home but there hadn't been time. She added, looking worried, that she just might have to spend the night at the Hallams. 'If so, I'll arrange for Hildy to sleep in the house with you. I'll send him home quite quickly. Now do get something to eat.'

Tom said there was no hurry. 'Actually, I rather

fancy going for a walk in the sunset. Don't you, Pam?' He gave her the kind of look that meant she should say 'yes', so she did, though she fully intended to have something to eat first.

'Well, if you go out, leave Hildy a note,' said Gram. 'I must take something to the Hallams.' She hurried into the kitchen and got a tinned ham and a large tin of fruit; then said, 'I *am* so sorry this should happen during your holiday.'

'It's just villages,' said Tom, philosophically. 'And you're what's known as the willing horse.'

'Not so willing at the moment. Oh, dear, I was so much looking forward to a happy evening with you.'

'There's still tomorrow,' said Pam.

'I hope so,' said Gram. 'Surely someone else can help out a bit? Anyway, don't worry about Miss Freke's birthday party. If I can't drive you to it, Hildy shall. Now I must dash.'

The twins saw her off. Then, even before the car was out of sight, Tom said:

'Now for Freke Hall! Come on, quick!' He raced back up the garden path.

Pam, racing after him, said, 'Tom! Are you crazy?'

'We're going there, at once. It's our last chance

to find the secret room. Tomorrow the builders will take over.'

'But we can't get into the house.'

'Yes, we can – through the kitchen window. I must write a note to Hildy.' He dived into the kitchen.

Pam, following him, said, 'But I can't walk all those miles.'

'You won't have to. We'll go across the fields. Twenty minutes to get there, twenty minutes in the house – if we need as much. Twenty minutes to get home. We can do the whole thing in an hour.'

'But it would mean crossing the old railway line. Gram said we mustn't.'

'She didn't absolutely forbid it. And she'd understand. If she hadn't had to rush off I'd have told her and she'd have driven us in the car. She's as keen as we are on finding the secret room.'

'We might not find it. I don't remember what Miss Freke said.'

'I do. Every word of it. To me, things like finding secret rooms are – well, like magic is, to you.' He finished writing his note. 'Oh, come on, Pam!'

She looked out of the window at the back of the kitchen. Already Freke Hall was dark against the golden western sky. She imagined climbing in, then going up the black back stairs to the Long Gallery. Suppose it got dark? She said, firmly, 'Sorry, Tom. I don't want to.'

'Then I must go alone. I've simply got to find the picture Miss Freke left there, and take it to her tomorrow.'

Pam hadn't thought of that. Now she imagined the picture, shut up for ninety years and needing to be rescued. She looked out of the window again and didn't feel any less frightened, but she knew she would have to go, not so much because of the picture and giving pleasure to Miss Freke as because she couldn't let Tom go alone. The fact that she was frightened made her all the more sure of this.

She said, 'Right. I'll get our wellington boots. There may be brambles on the railway banks.'

'And I'll get us some milk and some cake.'

Pam's appetite had gone but it came back while she ate and drank. She asked what he'd written to Hildy.

'Just that we'll be back in an hour or so.'

'I hope we shall,' said Pam. 'Will it be dark by then?'

'I shouldn't think so. Anyway, I'll take the kitchen torch. That's a good strong one.'

They went out of the back door to the back garden and then through the little gate that led to the bridge across the ditch. Already there was a faint chill in the windless evening air. The vast golden sunset was growing even vaster, enveloping everything in its light. Pam now felt more excited than frightened – or rather, she was managing to turn her fear into a kind of pleasure, such as she felt while watching anything exciting on television. She told herself, *It's an adventure. You like it, really.* But she still wasn't sure she did.

Tom's only fear was that the mechanism that moved the panel might no longer work, after ninety years. But it must, it must!

The going was easy at first, across a meadow. Then they came to a hedge hacked down to the ground and replaced by barbed wire which was awkward to get through; they were glad of their wellington boots. Then they were in a wheat field and had to walk round the edge of it. Then, at last, they reached the railway cutting.

It was deeper than they had remembered and the banks were now overgrown with weeds and brambles – several times Pam's dress got caught and it took time to disentangle it. When they got down to the old railway track they stood still, looking for the easiest place to scramble up the opposite bank.

'It's getting dark already,' said Pam.

'That's just because we're down here and can't see the sunset.' But it *was* getting darker quicker than he had expected.

'It feels eerie down here,' said Pam.

'Disused places often do. Look how peculiar disused buildings always seem on television.'

'Perhaps we'll see a ghost train,' said Pam, cheerfully. She was really quite enjoying the eeriness. Then she gasped and grabbed Tom's arm. 'Look!'

Around a quarter of a mile away were two bright lights, moving towards them.

'It must be a real train,' said Tom. 'Quick, get off the line.' Then, when they reached the bank, he added, 'But it can't be a real train. The rails have been taken up. It must be a car.'

'It's coming jolly fast and it's swaying. I should think it's being driven by someone drunk. Come on! I shouldn't like to meet anyone drunk down here.' Pam started to climb the bank.

'They probably haven't seen us,' said Tom, following her. 'Look out, you'll get torn to pieces.' She was plunging into a thicket of brambles. 'Just crouch down and keep still.'

The car, going faster than ever, drew nearer. It was really a small van. At the front were two people, roaring with laughter. One of them waved to the twins. The next instant the van was past, still swaying.

'How did they get on the track?' said Pam.

'Perhaps at the level crossing. The gates have gone. Keep still while I get you free from the brambles.'

'I feel like the ram in the thicket in that horrid bible story. I hope I have better luck than it did.'

Tom, while he freed her, took a quick glance at his watch. (Pam never wore one; she said her 'electricity' stopped watches. Tom thought she merely forgot to wind them.) Already the trip had taken half an hour, ten minutes longer than he'd reckoned would be needed to reach Freke Hall, and they still had another field to cross. But he was thankful to find that, when they got to the top of the bank, it seemed lighter, because the whole of the sunset was visible again. The gold was now deepening to flame, most beautiful but, to Pam, a little frightening. All that Tom thought about was getting to Freke Hall quickly.

The last field was easy. He said, 'Race you!' and they set off full tilt, but lost time when Pam tripped. As he helped her up she said, 'I was looking at the sunset. It seems a shame to waste it.'

They reached Freke Hall and hurried through the gates. But when the house was in sight Pam stopped dead. 'It's come back – all the scariness. It's worse now than before the bushes were cut down. It looks *menacing*.'

'Nonsense,' said Tom. 'Come on or I'll leave you behind.'

'Oh, no! Wait!' She raced after him.

They ran round to the back of the house. Suppose someone had closed the kitchen window? But it was still open. It was higher than Tom had remembered and he had a hard job to get Pam up, and a harder one to get himself up, without assistance, but at last they were in the kitchen.

'It's horrible,' said Pam. 'Suppose all those bells begin to clang?'

'Just follow the torch.' Tom lighted the way to the back stairs. 'I'll go first.' Then he changed his mind; he was none too sure she would follow him. 'No, you go first and I'll light you from behind.' He had to give her several shoves to get her to the first floor, where there was still a little daylight, coming through open doors. Now for the Long Gallery.

He had expected it to be flooded with sunset but only late twilight came through the recessed windows, and what little light there was seemed absorbed by the dark panelling. Still, he snapped the torch off. Its shaft of light confused him and he needed to get the feel of the room.

He led the way to the fireplace at the back of the room and looked to the left.

'Now!' he said. 'Three panels up and four left.'

The fourth panel was nearly in the corner of the room and almost in darkness. He would have to use his torch. Yes! There *were* three knots in the wood. He pressed the highest one.

Nothing happened.

'Miss Freke said you had to press *hard*,' Pam told him.

'I *am* pressing hard. You hold the torch.' He gave it to her, then said crossly, 'You're dazzling me. Shine it on the knot, not on my eyes.'

'Your hand's in the way,' said Pam. 'Anyway, the torch is modern. I think it interferes with the magic.' She snapped it off.

'It's not magic I'm counting on.' But he had his thumb firmly on the knot and could do without light. He pressed again, his very hardest. Still nothing happened. Perhaps his thumb wasn't strong enough. But if Miss Freke as a child had been able to work the spring, surely he could? Perhaps the mechanism was now immovable.

The knot was a fairly large one. He managed to get both his thumbs on it, thus doubling the pressure. And suddenly he heard a very slight whirring noise.

'There's something happening,' he cried.

Then Pam gave a little scream. 'Look, Tom, look.'

A few inches away from his thumbs was what looked like a long streak of fire. It gradually got wider. Only then he realised the panelling was moving, slowly swinging away from them. He could no longer keep his thumbs at full pressure but this now made no difference. The panelling went on swinging, right down to the ground, until it had provided an opening about eight inches wide. Then it stopped.

Tom, peering through the gap, saw a space around two feet wide and six feet long. And he now saw where the streak of fire had come from. In the brick wall of the narrow room was an opening like the arrow slits he had seen in the walls of castles, and the setting sun was shining through it.

'Can we get the panelling to open wider?' said Pam.

They tried but the panelling was immovable.

'Perhaps I can get through,' said Tom. He tried sideways, wiggling his behind.

'Don't get stuck!' Pam implored.

'No, I'm through all right.'

The little room seemed to be quite empty. Three of its walls were of brick, the fourth was the back of the panelling, on which Tom could see the metal mechanism that had opened the section of panelling. Nowhere could he see Miss Freke's painting. Then he noticed something pale, on the floor in one corner, and found it was a small package, tied up with ribbon. He had just picked it up when Pam cried, 'Tom! Quick! The panelling's closing.'

He dashed towards the opening. Already it was narrower. He threw the little package out, then grasped the edge of the panelling with both hands. He could feel it resisting him. He shouted to Pam, 'Fling your full weight against it,' and heard her do so, but the gap went on narrowing. He must try to get through what remained of it.

It was far more difficult than before. Then he had only had to press himself against the wood; now he could feel it pressing on him. There was a moment when he thought he would have to go back. And be shut in the secret room until Pam could get help? And where would she get it? There was no house anywhere near, and already it was nearly dark. She would never find her way back across the fields. In desperation he struggled even harder. Oh, glorious miracle! He was through!

Between them they had impeded the panelling's progress just a little. Now it moved on inexorably, and closed without leaving the slightest gap.

'Oh, gosh, how awful that was,' said Pam. 'I kept thinking –'

'Don't waste time on it. We've got to get home quickly.'

'Didn't you find any picture?'

'Only this.' He picked up the little package. 'Where's the torch?'

By its light they examined the package. It was wrapped up in pink silk and the ribbon with which it was tied was embroidered.

'Let's unwrap it now,' said Pam.

'No. I told you, we've got to get home.' He added, mentally, *If we can*. He didn't fancy getting Pam across the railway cutting with only a torch to guide them. 'Come on.'

It was at that moment that the Long Gallery was

suddenly brighter. They turned towards the fireplace at the far end. This was flanked by two tall windows, now quite dazzlingly bright. There was the noise of a car approaching. Then the windows grew dimmer. They heard the car draw up with a screech. Then its engine stopped.

They ran the full length of the Long Gallery and looked out of a window. They saw a small van, with two people at the front. The twins were instantly sure. It was the van they had seen careering past them on the old railway track.

7. GARY AND SANDRA AND KEVIN AND MARLENE AND LANCE AND MAUREEN

'They must have taken the wrong turning,' said Tom. 'They'll go away.'

But even as he spoke two men got out of the van and came towards the house. One of them had a black beard.

'They can't be the builders,' said Pam. 'Not at this time of night. They could be thieves.'

'There's nothing here to steal.'

'They may think there is. Paintings —'

Tom's grip on Miss Freke's little package tightened. *Could that be a valuable painting? But how could thieves know about it?* He said, 'I suppose they might steal the panelling.'

'Oh, Tom! They'll tie us up and gag us. They may even kill us – to stop us identifying them.'

'Of course they won't.' He meant to say it firmly but his voice shook. He had been badly frightened by his struggle to get out of the secret room and now he was smitten by guilt. He had persuaded Pam to come to Freke Hall; he had got her into this danger.

She gave him a quick, understanding look and then, as she sometimes could in an emergency, controlled herself and said briskly, 'Anyway, they're not going to catch us. We'll get out of the kitchen window and dodge them. It'll be quickest to go the front way.'

When they reached the Great Hall the men were already trying the front door.

Which way was the kitchen? Through the dining room, Pam remembered. It took a minute to find the right door, then they raced through into the dark passage. As they reached the kitchen Tom said, 'I'll get out of the window first and be ready to catch you. You'll have to sit on the sill and jump down.'

But as they ran towards the window the two men walked past, on their way to the back door.

'They'll see us if we get out now,' said Pam. 'We'll have to hide.'

'Where?'

'Anywhere to get away from them. That man with the black beard looked murderous.' She had seen it clearly in the last of the sunset. 'Come on!'

They dashed back through the long passage and into the dining room. Then, as they reached the Great Hall, Pam said, 'Stop! Listen!'

There was a thin, high-pitched wailing noise.

'It's some animal,' said Tom.

'No, it's not, it's a baby. And there's another – it sounds furious.' The second noise was a miniature roar. 'Oh, Tom, look!'

At the tall window of the Great Hall were two women, each with a baby in her arms.

'Oh, how marvellous!' cried Pam. 'Don't you understand, Tom? They're all squatters, not thieves. They often take over empty country houses.' She dashed back towards the kitchen. 'They'll be all right, if we're nice to them.'

Tom was not so sure of that. Still, one of the men had waved from the van, he now remembered; they might not be too bad. But as he raced after Pam he called, 'You said the one with the black beard looked murderous.'

'Oh, it's different if they're squatters.'

He reached the open window only a couple of seconds after her and they both leaned out. The men were now some distance away, past the back door. Pam called, 'Hello! We're in here and we're quite harmless.'

'Oh, my God!' said a man. 'Who are you? Where are you?' He shone a torch around until he located them.

'We're not the police or anything,' called Tom.

'They're just kids,' said the other man.

Tom now shone his own torch on the man. The one with the black beard no longer looked murderous; he just looked young. And the other man, who had long, fair side-whiskers, looked even younger.

'Stop blinding us,' said the bearded man.

'I will if you'll stop blinding us.' The torches were clicked off.

Pam said, in a voice suitable for a duchess, 'Let's all behave in a civilised way.' Then she added in her own voice, 'Anyway, we happen to be on your side.'

'Well, we were last night,' said Tom, 'when we saw some London squatters on television. Even our grandmother was quite sympathetic – well, a bit.'

'God bless your grandmother,' said the bearded

man. 'Is she in there with you?' Both men were now on their way to the window.

'No, we're quite on our own,' said Tom. 'And now we've got to get home.'

'Can you let us in before you go?' said the man with the side-whiskers.

Tom felt sure the vicar's wife wouldn't approve, but he followed Pam to the back door and turned the heavy key for her. She flung the door open and said, 'Welcome! Won't you bring the babies in?'

Even at this distance the wailing and the roaring could be heard.

'They always yell like that when they're wakened up before they want to be,' said the man with the side-whiskers. 'I'll go and get the girls.'

The bearded man called after him, 'And bring the lamp, will you, Kevin – and anything else you can carry?' Then he stood looking round the kitchen. 'Well, isn't this something!'

Pam said, 'I'm afraid it's no use your settling in because workmen are coming tomorrow to do the whole place up.'

The bearded man said Kev had heard that when he came down to size the house up for squatting. 'He saw a picture of it in a paper and took a fancy to it – had one of his feelings about it. And we thought the girls and the kids could do with some country air. We won't mind the workmen. Anyway, we'll try the place for a week or two.'

'But won't you get turned out?' asked Pam.

'You wait and see. We've got rights. And no one can say we broke in. Oh, we won't let anyone blame you for opening the door. We'll say we used that window.'

'Yes, it might be as well to leave us out of it,' said Tom. Gram might understand, but the vicar's wife wouldn't.

Voices were heard and then Kevin returned, bringing two young women and their babies, who had now stopped crying.

'Ah, your wives,' said Pam, politely.

'That's right,' said the bearded man. 'Sandra, here, is mine and Marlene is Kevin's.'

'And the babies' names?' Pam enquired.

'Ours is Maureen,' said Kevin's wife. She was fair, with long wispy hair and a great many scarves and beads. Both she and her baby were pretty.

'And this is Lance,' said the bearded man's wife. She was dark and plump – a bit plump for her jeans – but very handsome. So was her baby who already had quite a lot of black hair.

'I bet he's the one who roars,' said Pam.

'That's right,' said his mother, proudly.

Kevin had brought a large carton in which were a lamp, a kettle and an oil stove. He got the lamp lighted and it flared up with a strong white light and illuminated the whole kitchen.

'Will you look at that dresser?' said Sandra. 'A whole family could live in it. Pull a couple of the drawers out, Gary, and we'll put Lance and Maureen in.'

The babies, who looked extremely healthy, had suddenly gone to sleep. Their mothers padded the drawers with their shawls and popped them in.

'If you don't mind we'll go now,' said Tom. 'We've got a five mile walk ahead of us.' He turned to Pam. 'We can't go across the fields now. It wouldn't be safe.'

'It wouldn't be safe on the road, either, the speed cars come along,' said Gary. 'Tell you what, you give us a hand bringing our things in before it's quite dark and then I'll drive you home. All right?'

'Oh, yes, please!' said Pam.

Tom felt less enthusiastic, remembering the way the van had been driven along the old railway track. But it seemed the best thing to do. Already Hildy might be back and worrying about them.

Gary led the way to the van, then decided he could drive it round to the back door. He nearly overturned it on the way which caused both wives to scream loudly. With six of them on the job it took very little time to get everything indoors, including the television. 'Hope we get electricity for that soon,' said Gary. 'That is, if we like the set-up here.'

There were mattresses and sleeping bags – small ones for the babies – deck chairs and various bits of furniture, boxes and boxes of cooking utensils, provisions and clothes; also many colourful mats and draperies which Sandra and Marlene started spreading around at once.

'Leave that till tomorrow,' said Kevin. 'There are better rooms than this.'

But the girls said they liked the kitchen. 'There's the sink – and the pump handy,' said Marlene. 'And we might get that comic old range to work. I could fancy cooking a joint instead of frying sausages, sausages, sausages.'

'And our stuff'll look nice on the dresser.' Sandra was already setting out plates on it. 'Now, you drive the kids home, Gary – unless they'll stay to a sausage supper?'

'We should like to,' said Tom. 'But we've already been away much longer than we should have.'

Pam, too, would have liked to stay. She said, 'May we come back in our summer holidays – that is if you're still here?'

'Sure to be,' said Sandra. 'Though I doubt if we'll stick it through the winter – unless they put in central heating.'

'Might manage with log fires,' said Marlene. 'Do you know what, Kev? I've taken to it.'

'Said you would,' said Kevin, proudly.

He and Marlene and Sandra all came out to see the twins off and thanked them for their help. Marlene, gazing at the afterglow of sunset, said, 'Lovely, isn't it?'

'And later there'll be a moon,' said Tom.

'Yes, you get those in the country,' said Marlene. 'Nice.'

As Gary drove the van round to the front of the house, Pam suddenly cried, 'Oh, stop, please stop! Didn't you see it, Tom? One of our kittens – the white one!'

Gary had instantly braked. He said, 'I didn't see any kitten.'

'Nor I,' said Tom.

'It wasn't in front of the car. It was over there. Please let us get out and look.'

'Take your time,' said Gary.

Tom flashed his torch and saw a glimmer of white, but it turned out to be a large white stone. 'I suppose it *could* have been that,' said Pam. 'Or perhaps it turned itself into a stone.' She stooped and gave the stone a pat.

When they got back into the front of the van Gary was examining the package Tom had left on the seat.

'That's just a present for someone,' said Tom.

'The girls would have liked to see that embroidered ribbon. They collect that kind of thing.'

Pam said earnestly, 'Gary, if you should see a white kitten, if you should see *any* kittens, would you please spare them a little food?'

'Sure,' said Gary. 'If there's one thing we've got plenty of, it's cats' food. Lance is mad keen on it.'

'You don't mean you give cats' food to the babies?' said Pam.

'Sure. It's much better value than those fancy tins of baby food. Eat it ourselves sometimes. Very tasty on toast.'

Tom said, 'I don't think we should talk too much,

Pam. We might distract Gary from his driving. Turn left here, Gary.'

What worried Tom most on the way home was that, if they were found dead on the road, Gram would think they had broken one of her strictest rules and accepted a lift while out walking. But in spite of the speed at which Gary drove and the ominous noises made by the van, they reached Himbers safely. It was in darkness.

Tom said, 'If we get out quickly and put the lights on, we shan't have to explain why we were out after dark. Our grandmother doesn't like us to be.'

'Well, it's been nice knowing you,' said Gary. 'Come and see us again. And bring your grandmother, if she approves of squatters.'

Pam said, 'We ought to mention that she doesn't approve of *all* squatters.'

'Neither do we, mate. That's partly why we're here – to get away from some of them. Now in you go.'

'Thank you for driving us home,' said Pam.

'It was a pleasure,' said Gary, and was off.

They raced into the house and put all the downstairs lights on, then got their wellington boots off and started preparations for supper, in Gram's spick and span kitchen.

'I keep seeing the kitchen at Freke Hall now the squatters are in it,' said Pam. 'It looked fun.'

'I thought so, too,' said Tom. 'I wonder if Gram's got any sausages we can have for supper.'

They had the table laid and sausages in the frying pan by the time Hildy got back, driving the car.

He said, 'Your gram can't come. Miss Hallam's back's real bad. She's got to go and have it X-rayed tomorrow. And the old people will have to go into a hospital and stay there for a while, your gram says. She's going to see them through the night – I'm to sleep indoors with you – and then she and the doctor hope to get everything fixed tomorrow. I'm to drive you to Miss Freke's party.'

'Poor Gram, she must be terribly tired,' said Pam. 'And you look tired, Hildy. Sit down. We'll get the supper.'

'I must make up my bed here.'

'We'll do that, while you get your things for the night.'

There was a room off the kitchen which Hildy and his wife had used before the cottage had been done up for them. Hildy still used it whenever he was ill and Gram felt he needed nursing.

Later, Gram rang up, full of apologies and saying

they must enjoy their outing with Hildy next day. 'He'll take you to lunch at the place we went to today – I've given him money. And don't let him worry about the prices. I'll hope to be home before you get back as I've fixed with someone to look after Mary if they don't keep her in hospital – which I think they will; apart from her back she's on the edge of a nervous breakdown. But you're not to worry about anything.'

Tom, who had answered the telephone, assured her they wouldn't. 'We'll just look forward to our last evening together.' Then he added in a very grown-up tone, 'Try not to tire yourself too much.'

'Oh, I'm not tired,' said Gram, untruthfully. 'Tell Miss Freke how sorry I am not to meet her. And take her some flowers. I've asked Hildy to gather some for her. Goodnight, darling. Love to Pam.'

Tom had said he would not worry but, actually, he was worried already. Again they had been prevented from telling Gram about the kittens.

He consulted Pam. Should they now tell Hildy? But apart from his lack of enthusiasm about cats, they did not feel they could ask him to stay up till midnight, to see the kittens. He was already tired and he had a long drive ahead of him next day. They started urging him to bed soon after ten o'clock.

He saw them preparing bread and milk for the hedgehogs and said two hedgehogs couldn't eat so much. 'And you'll attract rats if you're not careful – or stray cats.'

'What's wrong with stray cats?' said Pam. 'Mogg was a stray cat once.'

'Mogg was different.' He had, indeed, loved Mogg, when she was not damaging his garden. 'Well, goodnight, my dears. I'll be here if you want me. Just knock on my door.'

At eleven o'clock they put out the bread and milk and watched from above. Again the hedgehogs came first and ate so much that, again, Pam wanted to scare them off. She said, 'It isn't as if they depend on the bread and milk. Hedgehogs eat all sorts of things.'

Tom said, 'It's hard on the hedgehogs. We'd love them dearly if it wasn't for the kittens.'

'Well, I do love them dearly, but I love the kittens more.'

Tom himself was thinking he might have to scare them, when they suddenly scuttled off, leaving plenty of bread. He was able to refill the dishes with milk from his glass, and Pam's. Then they sat on the window seat waiting for midnight.

'I wonder how the squatters are getting on,' said Tom.

'I expect they're all asleep in the sleeping bags. The babies will look sweet in theirs.'

'The builders are going to get a bit of a shock tomorrow. But I daresay they won't mind, especially if the girls make them lots of cups of tea. I'm glad it's hard to get squatters out.'

'The vicar's wife won't be pleased,' said Pam.

'Oh, she'll fall for the babies. So will Gram. Goodness, I wish she was here with us, watching. Let's try hard tonight to see where the kittens come from.'

When the church clock struck midnight the lilac tree was in full moonlight, its blossoms shining white.

'No kittens,' said Tom.

'Give them a chance. The church clock's probably fast.'

But two minutes, seeming much longer, passed and there were still no kittens. And then –

They were suddenly there, not under the lilac tree but below the window, hurrying towards the bread and milk.

'They fooled us,' whispered Pam, delightedly.

125

'They knew we were watching the lilac tree. They don't *want* us to know where they come from.'

Again the kittens cleared one dish before turning to the other. But tonight they cleared that, too, and then went back to the first dish to see if they had left anything. Their little tongues licked in vain.

'Oh, they haven't had enough,' wailed Pam. 'We must get them some more from the kitchen. Quick!'

'I'm afraid we might wake Hildy.'

'Never mind that. They're hungry. I can't bear them to be hungry.'

But at that moment all four kittens dashed away, without so much as washing their faces. Tom thought they might have heard Pam's voice but he wasn't going to say so. Instead he said, 'They've really had quite a lot. But it does make one realise they'll want more and more as they grow bigger. Whatever happens tomorrow we've simply got to tell Gram.'

8. MISS FREKE'S KITTENS

The next morning Hildy gathered a collection of summer flowers from his herbaceous border, wrapped their stems in damp cotton wool and put them in a basket. The twins decided to put the package from the secret room under them, protected by a plastic bag. They didn't want Hildy to see it before they'd had a chance to tell Gram about last night's trip to Freke Hall.

They resisted the temptation to open the packet, because they both felt it should still be intact when they gave it to Miss Freke. The pink silk it was wrapped in felt as if there were many layers; they could only just feel that there was something hard inside.

'It must be a very small picture,' said Pam. She stroked the ribbon that tied up the packet. It was embroidered with daisies and had a narrow, looped edging. 'I wonder if it was one of her hair ribbons? You often see children with hair ribbons in old picture books.'

Gram rang up just before they were ready to leave, to tell them her plans for the Hallams were going well and she felt sure she would be home when they got back. Then she told them to hurry up and start off as she knew Hildy would not want to drive fast.

They soon found that Hildy was nervous. He asked them to sit at the back, in case their conversation distracted him. He had once been an excellent driver but, of recent years, had done little more than drive backwards and forwards to the village. Gram had supplied him with written instructions for the later part of the journey, but had taken it for granted he would know his way for a considerable distance. He no longer remembered it well and the further afield he got, the worse things were. When they reached the hotel where they were to lunch, the dining room had closed and they had to find somewhere else. The twins would willingly have skipped lunch, but Hildy said he needed a rest.

It was a poor lunch and a slow one. By the time they were back in the car it was half-past three. They were due at Miss Freke's party at four and they now had the most difficult part of the journey ahead of them, through many little lanes. Gram's instructions were now detailed but, again and again, Hildy went wrong. At last Tom asked if he might sit in front and read out the instructions. Hildy was a bit touchy about this, but finally agreed and then they got on better. But it was just on five o'clock when they at last reached the nursing home.

'Tea parties usually go on till five – and after,' said Pam, hopefully.

But that had not been the case with Miss Freke's tea party. The nurse in the hall told them it was over. 'We thought you weren't coming. We've just left her to take a nap.'

When they explained what had happened, the nurse said she would tiptoe in and see if Miss Freke was still awake.

'If she is, please tell her we've brought her a present,' said Tom.

'Lovely flowers,' said the nurse.

'Not just flowers,' said Pam. 'It's something from Freke Hall, something we *know* she'll want.'

'If we can't see her, I suppose we'll have to leave it for her,' said Tom.

But the nurse returned to say they could have just

a few minutes with Miss Freke. 'Not more, because she's got to be fresh for this evening, to see herself on television. You wouldn't believe all the goings on this morning.'

This time Miss Freke's room looked very different. The curtains, green satin, were drawn and were heavy enough to shut out much of the light. The birdcage was covered. All the gaiety had been replaced by a gentle dimness, and Miss Freke no longer looked lively. But she gave them each a smile and held out her hands to them. She was not lying down, just lying back against her pillows. Instead of her high, frilled cap she was now wearing a soft white bonnet tied under her chin in a bow.

She had been told about the difficulties of the journey and they now explained why their grandmother hadn't come. Miss Freke said she was so very sorry they had missed the party. She had already asked the nurse to pack them a piece of the cake to take away with them.

'Such a lovely party it was, with my kind nurses. It would have gone on longer if I hadn't got a little tired – oh, not by the party; it was the television, this morning, that started it. My dears, it was quite alarming. This room was *packed* with people, and cameras and wires and lights, such hot, glaring lights. Somehow I feel my room has been *hurt*. All the peace has been shattered.'

'It doesn't feel like that to us,' said Tom. 'It feels very restful.'

'And I'm sure the peace will come back for you before long,' said Pam.

'I doubt it,' said Miss Freke. 'And I doubt if I shall ever feel quite the same about television. It never occurred to me before that when you see a beautiful, quiet scene, there are all those men and cameras just out of sight.'

'It never occurred to me either,' said Tom. 'And anyway, I don't think it matters. When one's looking at a painting, one doesn't worry because there was once an artist standing in front of it, with his palette. Which reminds me –' He stooped and picked up the basket. Pam lifted out the flowers and he dived down and got the silk-wrapped packet. 'Is this your hidden picture, Miss Freke?'

She gave a little gasp and sank back against her pillows. But before the twins had time to feel anxious about her she smiled sweetly at them. 'You marvellous children! Give it to me, give it to me! That was my hair ribbon and that was my best silk sash. And now I remember just what's inside. Undo it for me, please.'

Tom untied the ribbon and Pam removed the sash. There were many folds of it. The silk was thick and soft like no material Pam had ever felt before. The picture, at last revealed, was not much bigger than a miniature. It had a frame covered with tiny pink shells. But it was the painting itself which made Pam gasp.

It was of four kittens, against a green background. The green must have been intended for grass as there were flowers in it, but the painter had not understood about perspective so the top two kittens appeared to be floating above the heads of the bottom two. There was one white kitten, one black kitten, one ginger kitten and one tabby kitten.

'My dear kittens!' murmured Miss Freke.

'But they're ours, too,' gasped Pam. 'They come at midnight. They're exactly like yours, aren't they, Tom?'

Tom studied them while Pam, in a welter of words, explained to Miss Freke. It was true that the colours of the kittens resembled the midnight kittens, but the painted kittens were not really like *any* kittens. They were too badly painted. But they had large eyes and very fine whiskers and they certainly had a kittenish look.

Pam, reaching the end of her breathless story, said, 'Could our kittens be the descendants of your kittens?'

Miss Freke smilingly shook her head. 'I'm afraid not, my dear, because I painted them from imagination. There were no cats or kittens at Freke Hall and I did so long for some. My aunt gave me that very pretty frame and I think I valued it even more than the painting. Now, of course, I value them equally – and the sash and the ribbon. They are *me*, ninety years ago.'

Tom began to tell her how they had followed her instructions and found the secret room. Then he stopped, because he saw she was not listening. She was gazing, with smiling eyes, as if at a vision. Was she seeing the past, he wondered – or was she right back in the past? He looked at Pam and saw her part her lips as if to speak, then close them again. They both waited silently until the visionary look faded from Miss Freke's eyes and she was, once more, just a pleasantly smiling old lady.

'Dear children,' she said. 'You have given me a very wonderful present.'

The door opened and the nurse came in. She looked quickly at Miss Freke, then said, 'Time to go, children.'

'Oh, they haven't tired me,' said Miss Freke. 'Still, I think I should rest now. Goodbye, my dears. But wait! There's something I want to tell you, if I can find the words.' She was silent for a moment, then she went on. 'Then and now are the same, always have been and always will be. I don't suppose you can understand that now. But you may, one day.'

'I think I understand now,' said Pam.

Tom, after a moment's hesitation, said, 'I think I *almost* understand.'

Then they said goodbye and the nurse hurried them out of the room. At the door she said, 'Wait for me downstairs. I shan't be long,' and went back to Miss Freke.

After they had waited downstairs for over five minutes, Tom said, 'Do you think we tired Miss Freke? I thought the nurse looked a bit worried.'

'*I* thought we did Miss Freke good,' said Pam. 'Her cheeks got such a pretty pink flush.'

'Perhaps ladies who are a hundred years old aren't supposed to have flushed cheeks.'

But when the nurse came back she said they hadn't harmed Miss Freke. 'I just waited to make sure she was resting peacefully. She's asleep now – still holding the little picture. Do try to see her on television tonight. They said she would be on the news.'

Then the nurse gave them quite a large piece of the birthday cake to take away and saw them off.

They found Hildy asleep at the wheel of the car; he had intended to walk round the gardens, but had felt too tired. When they woke him he looked so dazed that they asked if he would like to get some tea somewhere, but he said he wanted to hurry home. So Tom cut the birthday cake into three pieces with his pocket knife, for them to share. On the way back Tom sat with Hildy, directing him, so they only got lost once.

Pam, at the back, thought what a strange coincidence it was that they had met Miss Freke on the day after they went over to Freke Hall. Pam loved coincidences; surely they were a little bit magic? And then Miss Freke had been able to tell them how to find the secret room the day after they searched for it. Was that a coincidence, too? In a way; though it was more a link in a chain. But the strangest coincidence, the strangest link, was that Miss Freke's kittens were the midnight kittens. Surely *that* must be magic?

Miss Freke, as a child, had painted her kittens from imagination. If you imagined things well enough, could you bring them to life – and if you did, would they be alive for ever? And Miss Freke had said that then and now were the same. Pam had felt she understood that, but now the meaning was drifting away from her. And soon she fell asleep.

9. WHY ARE YOU INVENTING THIS NONSENSE?

By the time they got home it was raining; not hard, just a depressing drizzle. But there were lights on and, even from the road, the twins could see a flicker which told them that Gram had lit the dining room fire. They dashed in, while Hildy put the car away.

Tom explained why they were so late and warned Gram that Hildy was pretty tired. She had laid a place for him in the dining room and intended them all to have a festive supper, but she guessed he might prefer to go to bed. She suggested it as soon as he came in and he agreed without protest, and also agreed to spend another night in the kitchen bedroom and have his supper in bed.

'We'll wait on you, Hildy,' said Tom, eagerly. As well as wanting to be kind he would be glad to have Hildy out of the way while they told Gram about the kittens. And tell her they now must, even before supper. He said so to Pam, while Gram was urging Hildy to bed.

When she came back Tom asked, very politely, about the Hallams. She said firmly, 'They're all right and we're not going to say one word about them. This is *your* evening. Now tell me about Miss Freke.'

'We've something more important to tell you about first,' said Tom. 'Would you mind sitting down by the fire?'

'And have a glass of sherry,' said Pam.

Gram laughed. 'That sounds like a bribe. But I really think I will. The casserole won't be ready for a little while.'

Tom got the sherry while Pam brought a footstool – which was something Gram never used, but she valued the attention. What did the twins want to tell her? Perhaps they wanted to ask for something, which they very seldom did. *Well, if they do*, she thought, relaxing in her chair, *I shall probably give it to them, right up to the half of my kingdom*. Which was, she realised, a foolish thought, seeing that they, themselves, represented at least ninety per cent of her kingdom. And what the remaining ten per cent was she couldn't for the moment think.

'Now!' she said encouragingly.

The twins looked at each other. Then Tom said, 'You first, Pam.'

Pam said, slowly for her, even haltingly, 'It's just that we've got four kittens.'

'How do you mean, got them?' said Gram.

Pam looked at Tom for help. He said, 'They come to share the hedgehogs' bread and milk. They've come every night since we got home.'

Pam, now with a burst of speed, said, 'They don't exactly come, they appear. They're suddenly there, under the lilac tree, on the stroke of midnight, except one night when the church clock must have been fast. And then they dance in the moonlight, do a kind of ballet, most magical –'

Gram interrupted. 'Darling, you mean they're pretend kittens, like the tiger and the snake?'

'No, no!'

Tom said, very gravely, 'I'm afraid they're quite real, Gram. And very hungry. That's why we have to tell you about them. They need to be fed. They'll need far more than the hedgehogs get.'

'But why haven't you told me before?'

139

Together the twins explained. They'd tried to tell her at breakfast on Saturday, but she'd said so firmly she didn't want another cat; and they weren't sure the kittens would come again – but they had. And then, on Sunday morning, she'd gone to the village before they were up. And they hadn't felt they could tell her during the outing to the nursing home in case it spoilt the day for her – and on the way back, she'd asked them not to distract her by talking to her. And as soon as they got home she'd gone off to the village until now. This was their first real chance. Did she *understand?*

'Yes, yes, of course,' she said, troubled by their anxiety. 'It's been *my* fault, really. And they came again last night?'

'And wanted more food than there was.' Tom knelt down beside her chair and looked up with troubled eyes. 'Gram, you wouldn't, you couldn't . . .' His words trailed away.

'Couldn't what?'

'Well, Cook at school said most people feel wild kittens should be put to sleep.'

'And you were afraid that I –' Now she understood the fear in his eyes. '*Of course* I wouldn't think of such a thing. We'll just have to cope with them, find them homes . . .' But even as she said it she remembered how often there were village kittens in need of homes, and not wild kittens but the offspring of much cherished pets. 'Oh, we'll manage somehow. They'll soon need other food besides bread and milk . . . What's the matter, Tom?'

He had sighed deeply and leaned his head against her knee. 'It's just the relief.' Oh, wonderful Gram! How could he have feared she would ever be less than wonderful? He looked up at her and smiled.

'He's been more worried than I have,' said Pam. 'Because *I* believe they are magic kittens, which means that *something* will take care of them. But magical creatures do need food – think of all the fairy feasts.'

Gram said, 'They've probably been eating the hedgehogs' bread and milk for some time and that's why their mother felt she could leave them here. It seems heartless the way mother cats suddenly leave their kittens, but I suppose it's a law of nature. Now get ready for supper, darlings, while I take a tray to Hildy. And *don't worry any more.*'

While they were upstairs Pam said, 'We haven't told her about going to Freke Hall and crossing the railway line. That's quite a bit on my conscience.

And she won't like it that we were driven home by the squatters.'

'Let's try to lay off it until after supper. I want to enjoy Gram's casserole.'

According to the twins, casseroles could be deadly dull or extremely exciting. The dull kind were pale, watery and with all their ingredients instantly spottable. The exciting kind were dark and mysterious. Tonight, Gram's casserole was so dark that Tom said admiringly, 'Did you colour it with coal?' And try as they might the twins could not spot what was giving it a special flavour. What with eating it and talking about it, no other subject was mentioned until they were well into second helpings, when Gram said, 'But you haven't told me about your tea party. Hildy was worried that you arrived so late for it.'

'I think he needs new spectacles,' said Tom.

Gram sighed. 'He's just had some and a special pair for driving. The trouble is he finds it hard to concentrate on anything but gardening and little household jobs. I'll just see if he'd like seconds.'

While she was gone, Tom said, 'Let's not talk about Miss Freke or we shall have to mention the picture we took to her and how we got it.'

'But isn't not talking about it a bit like acting a lie?'

'Not if we intend to tell her later. Though I'm not quite sure we need.'

'But if we don't, it'll be real deception, seeing how important it was to us. Besides, I want to link up Miss Freke's kittens with our kittens. It's all part of the magic.'

Tom said, 'You do realise Miss Freke's kittens weren't real?'

'She might have forgotten them – or created them by imagining them and they've been waiting to be born.'

'That's an idiotic idea,' said Tom, brusquely. But he doubted if he'd made any impression on her.

When Gram came back she brought fruit salad and cream, and said Hildy now seemed quite himself. 'I must just make sure he doesn't do jobs that worry him. He's got to the age when he needs a bit of mothering.'

'What we need,' said Tom, 'is someone to mother *you*.'

'Wait till the summer holidays,' said Pam. 'Then we'll be a father and a mother to you.'

'You were going to tell me about Miss Freke's party,' said Gram.

Then the telephone rang. Gram, guessing it would be the vicar's wife, went upstairs to take it. The twins would not enjoy keeping quiet for what might be a long conversation.

'Saved by the bell,' said Tom, which they both thought very funny, though Pam was now longing to tell all about finding the painting.

They finished their fruit salad and lingered over their Coca Cola in wine glasses. Then Tom remembered that Miss Freke might be on the news.

'Oh, goodness, we've missed it,' said Pam.

'Not if it comes at the very end of the news, as that kind of thing often does. Let's see.'

They ran into the sitting room and switched on the television. The voices came through at once and they realised the news was still in progress. 'Oh, hurry up, picture!' said Pam. Then the newscaster said, 'And finally we bring you a glimpse of a lady whose hundredth birthday has the charm of a fairy tale.'

'It's her!' cried Pam. 'Look!'

The picture began forming, uncertainly at first, then it steadied. They saw the cake with its hundred candles. Tom dashed to the foot of the stairs and called up, 'Gram, come quickly! Miss Freke's on TV.'

But Gram's bedroom door was closed. Then Pam called, 'Come back, Tom. You're missing it.'

He got back in time to see Miss Freke's room, with its many little pictures, bowls of flowers, birdcage; and then the camera focussed on Miss Freke. She was sitting up against her lace-covered pillows, wearing her lace bed-jacket, muslin ruff, and lace bonnet with its high, pleated frill. From above, the green chiffon draperies descended from the silver crown. It was a setting for the Sleeping Beauty.

And Miss Freke herself? She had said there would be little of her to be seen –'Just the bit between my bonnet and my ruff, and the tips of my fingers.' And it seemed to the twins that there was even less of her face to be seen than in real life. Two dark, sunken eyes, a tiny, pointed nose – 'Goodness,' said Pam. 'She's like our hedgehogs. But they look sadder than she does.'

Miss Freke certainly didn't look sad. She smiled, and the smile illuminated her whole face. Then she said, in her tiny, tinkling voice, 'I've had such a happy birthday. I hope you will all live to be a hundred and be as happy as I am.' Then she raised a lace-mittened hand and waved, as a child waves, and said, 'My love to you all.'

The picture faded. The newscaster was back. He said, 'And I'm sure many of us would like to send our love to her.'

Gram came down just in time to hear the last words. 'You've missed Miss Freke,' wailed Pam. 'I bet you were talking to the vicar's wife. That frightful woman!'

'Pam, darling!' Gram protested, then added, 'Well, perhaps she was just a little bit frightful tonight. I mean, we've lived through two days of the Hallams troubles. We didn't need to talk our way all through them again. Tell me about the broadcast while I finish my fruit salad and then I'll make us some hot chocolate.'

When they had cleared the table Tom went to get Hildy's tray. 'Did Miss Freke have lots of lovely presents?' said Gram, as she and Pam stacked the dishwasher.

'She didn't show us any. I wish our little picture had arrived earlier. Then it might have been on television.'

Gram looked puzzled. 'What little picture?'

Even though Pam was eager to tell the whole story, both to get it off her conscience and share the adventure with Gram, she hadn't meant to start on it without Tom. She waited a second, hoping he would come back, but she could hear him talking to Hildy. At last she plunged in. 'Well, it was hidden in the secret room at Freke Hall. There really is one. Miss Freke told us how to find it and we did.'

Gram was now looking utterly bewildered. 'But you can't have. There hasn't been time.'

'Yes, there was – last night. It had to be then so we could get the picture in time for Miss Freke's birthday.'

'Are you telling me you walked all those miles to Freke Hall?'

If only Tom would come back! It had been his idea that they should go by the fields, but she wasn't going to put all the blame on him. She said, 'Oh, it didn't take long. We went, well, direct.'

'You crossed the old railway line?'

'You didn't absolutely forbid it, did you?'

Tom came back with Hildy's tray. Pam went on brightly, 'I've been telling Gram about our finding the secret room.'

'Ah,' said Tom. He wished he knew what she'd said. The great thing was to treat the matter casually, not make too much importance of it. He wasn't afraid that Gram would be angry; she never was.

But she might be upset that they'd done something she'd asked them not to. And it would be specially dreadful to upset her now, when she'd been so wonderful about the kittens.

Pam went on, 'We did wish you'd been with us, Gram. It was terrible exciting.'

'But the Hall must have been locked up. Good heavens, you didn't break in, did you?'

'Oh, no, there was a window open. Tom happened to see it when we went to the Hall with you.'

Gram noticed Tom was not joining in the conversation. Perhaps his conscience was troubling him. Well, she mustn't make too much of the matter. Considering that she, herself, would have liked to find the secret room, she could hardly blame the twins for jumping at a real chance to find it. Strange how most children were fascinated by the idea of secret rooms. Pam was now pouring out details which might have come from any number of stories for children. Gram's mind gave a lurch. Could they *be* from some story? She said, 'Pam, darling, this really did happen? You're not fooling your old grandmother?'

'Of course not!' said Pam, and went on to describe how the panelling started to close and she and Tom fought with it. 'But first he threw Miss Freke's painting out – imagine, it had been there ninety years. And, Gram, it's a painting of four kittens, *exactly* like ours.'

'That reminds me,' said Tom. 'I'll get their food ready.' If only Pam would stop now! She still hadn't mentioned the squatters and the ride home in Gary's van.

Gram, now making the chocolate, began to feel really suspicious. Tom had still made no comment on the trip to Freke Hall and she rather thought he had deliberately changed the conversation. She poured the chocolate into mugs and took one in to Hildy, closing his door behind her. Setting the mug down on the bedside table she said, 'Hildy, did you see the picture the twins took to Miss Freke?'

'There wasn't any picture,' said Hildy. 'Only the flowers, in a basket.'

Gram, suddenly hating herself for questioning Hildy, said, 'The picture must have been under them – Pam did say it was a small one. I'll say goodnight now.'

'Be up early in the morning, I will, to get you all off to the station. I'm a fraud, really, lying in bed being waited on.'

'Got to take care of you – seeing how you usually take care of me. Sleep well, dear Hildy.'

Going back to the kitchen she deliberately discarded her suspicions. If Pam had been romancing, Tom would have shut her up. And there was nothing impossible in Pam's story. She would get some more details later.

Tom had now filled the dishes with bread and loaded them, with a big jug of milk, on to a tray with the mugs of chocolate. 'Let's see what's on television,' he said brightly. Anything to stop Pam chattering. However, he'd just asked her not to mention squatters and she'd said she'd try not to. He wanted Gram to fall in love with the kittens before anything upset her.

They settled in front of the television and drank their chocolate. Tom eventually found a programme they all quite liked. But after she had set her mug down, Gram closed her eyes and fell asleep.

'We'll have to wake her at midnight,' Pam whispered.

'It's nowhere near midnight yet. Let her sleep. She probably didn't get any sleep at all last night, nursing three Hallams.'

'You'd think the television would wake her.'

'I suppose if you can fall asleep during a noise, you can stay asleep. Still, I'll turn the sound down a bit.'

Soon after that the programme changed to a play about ghosts. Pam adored anything about ghosts. Tom did not, because he didn't believe in ghosts and could never get interested in anything he didn't believe in. So he sat back and thought his own thoughts. He wished now that he'd told Gram about the squatters. After all, he and Pam weren't to blame for the squatters and, in the circumstances, their ride home in the van was quite excusable; and he needn't *stress* how dangerous it had been. Gram would understand. He'd tell her now if she hadn't fallen asleep but he wasn't going to wake her. He tried to get interested in the ghost play but found it made him sleepy. That wouldn't do at all — suppose he slept past midnight? He looked at his watch — still quarter of an hour to wait.

He got up and went to the french window. How dark it was outside! He had counted on a moon. He tiptoed off to get the kitchen torch. As he returned, midnight was striking. It was merely part of the ghost story on television, but it brought Pam back to earth with a bump. She sprang up crying, 'Oh, Tom, we'll have missed the kittens.'

Tom reassured her that it wasn't midnight yet but added, 'Still, I think we might wake Gram now.'

But Pam's cry had already done that.

'Oh, dear,' said Gram, 'I always feel so guilty when I sleep in front of the television.'

'You've woken up just at the right time,' said Tom. 'We can put the hedgehogs' dishes out now and, if they come, we can refill the dishes for the kittens.'

He poured the milk on to the two dishes of bread, while Pam watched the end of her television play. 'I'd guessed it, really,' she said, then helped carry the dishes to the french window. Gram, yawning, followed with the torch.

As soon as they were outside they realised it was raining, quietly but steadily. It had rained as they drove back from the nursing home, but cleared up during the evening and none of them knew it had started again.

'Do hedgehogs mind rain?' said Pam.

'I don't know,' said Gram. 'But the kittens certainly will.'

'Ours won't,' said Pam, confidently.

'Anyway, I wouldn't put the dishes out now, darlings, or they'll fill with rain.'

'But we can't disappoint the hedgehogs,' said Tom. 'We've got more milk for the kittens.'

'All right,' said Gram. 'But come in now. This is very wetting rain.'

Tom stood just inside the french window and shone the torch into the orchard. The rain became much heavier. 'It's just silver stair rods,' he said. 'I can't see any distance at all.' Gram said, 'I assure you, the kittens won't come in this downpour.'

'Wait till midnight,' said Pam.

Gram looked at her watch. 'It's midnight now.'

'The church clock hasn't struck.'

'We shouldn't hear it in this downpour. Close the window, Tom. I really think we should go to bed.'

'No, no, no!' cried Pam. 'They *must* come. Perhaps they're by the lilac tree.' She snatched the torch from Tom and dashed into the orchard.

'Pam, come back!' Gram shouted.

'I'll get her,' said Tom, dashing after her.

It was several minutes before they returned.

'Now you really must go to bed,' said Gram. 'You're wet through.'

'I really don't think they'll come tonight,' said Tom.

'Then they'll die of starvation – or drown.'

Tom, though he was himself harrowed at the thought of hungry, wet kittens, said firmly, 'They won't starve in one night. And they may have found somewhere to shelter.'

A light of hope dawned in Pam's eyes. 'Tom, do you think they could all be at Freke Hall? You know I saw the white one there last night. If they *are* there, the squatters will feed them.'

'What squatters?' said Gram.

'There were four of them,' said Pam, eagerly. 'Gary and Sandra and Kevin and Maureen. All very nice. And two sweet baby squatters who get given cat food. They were asleep in the dresser drawers. And just before Gary drove us home I saw our white kitten, only it turned into a stone.'

'Stop, stop!' said Gram, her thoughts whirling. 'Why are you inventing this nonsense?'

'I'm not inventing anything,' said Pam, indignantly.

'But you must be, darling.' Gram was now convinced that not only the squatters were invented. The walk across the fields, the secret room, Miss Freke's picture . . .

Pam said, 'Are you accusing me of lying?'

'Not lying, exactly. But, well, making things up. Like the tiger and the snake.'

'The tiger was ages ago.'

'The snake wasn't,' said Gram.

Pam took a deep breath, then said, 'The snake was true. I did it to save its life.'

'I didn't know that,' said Tom.

'I didn't want to put it on your conscience as well as mine. It's the only real lie I've ever told you, Gram. And I'm not lying now.'

'But some of the things you've described –'

'Perhaps you think I've invented the kittens,' said Pam, bitterly.

'No, not the kittens.' Tom also had spoken of the kittens. Gram felt safe about that. But he hadn't said one word about anything else. She turned to him now and was astonished to see that he was glaring at her. 'Tom, what is it?'

'I think you should believe my sister,' said Tom.

He spoke in a tone she had never heard him use before, forceful, almost grim. And the expression in his eyes was strange. He was, actually, furious that Pam's word was being doubted, but Gram, who had never before seen him angry, didn't realise that. Her best guess was that he was trying to convey something to her, hint, perhaps, that for the moment, she should accept what Pam said. Pam was certainly worked up about the kittens. Anyway, the tension must be resolved. *And it's up to me to do it*, thought Gram.

She said, 'Of course I believe you, Pam.'

'You don't mean that,' said Pam. 'Tom, would you kindly assure her everything I've said is true?'

'Certainly,' said Tom, coldly. 'I'd better start with the kittens. Then there's the walk to Freke Hall, and finding the secret room and Miss Freke's picture, and then the squatters and the ride home in their van. The only thing I didn't see that Pam saw was the white kitten at Freke Hall. But I did see the white stone. Anything else you'd like to know, Gram? Though I can't see why you should believe me when you don't believe Pam.'

'But I do believe her, I believe both of you.' But now she believed neither of them. She was convinced that, for some reason, Tom had decided he must support his sister. Could Pam be on the edge of a nervous breakdown, confusing imagination with reality? But, if so, why hadn't Tom told her? The great thing now was to get away from the children before she did any more damage – she was too tired to think sensibly. She said, 'Now I think we should all go to bed. But first we'll have one more look for the kittens.' Those kittens she now no longer believed in. Well, she never had believed they came on the dot of midnight.

Tom opened the french window. It was still pouring. The food was swamped. He said, 'Perhaps the hedgehogs will eat it.'

'While the kittens die of starvation or drown in a ditch,' said Pam.

'Oh, pull yourself together,' said Tom, fairly

brusquely. 'You've been saying nothing could go wrong with them because they're magic kittens.'

'They're not all that magic,' said Pam. She gave a great gulp of tears and ran upstairs.

'I'd better go after her,' said Tom. 'Goodnight, Gram.'

She longed to call him back, but felt sure she would only make matters worse. If he'd wanted to tell her anything he could have done so now.

'I'm too tired,' she thought, 'too tired to think any more.' Perhaps tomorrow she would be able to accept Pam's fantastic story, but she doubted if she ever would; and Tom's stilted confirmation of it had made her feel even more doubtful. She'd told them she accepted it, but she didn't think they believed her.

It was the first time in their lives that they had ganged up in opposition to her. Why? Why?

It was the first time in their lives that their much-loved grandmother had failed them. Tom, seeing his sister through an out of control fit of sobbing, heard himself thinking, *This is double trouble*. He might put on a brave face about the kittens, but he was as anxious about them as Pam was. On top of which, Gram believed he and Pam were lying. Never again could he count on her. He was shattered with loss.

10. A TELEPHONE RINGS AFTER MIDNIGHT

Long before their grandmother telephoned, Mike knew there was something wrong with the twins.

On the day the school got back from the half-term holiday there was to be an afternoon gathering to discuss the outing in London, the previous Friday. Soon after lunch the twins asked to be excused from this, saying they wanted to go for a long walk.

Normally, he would have agreed without any questions. If children didn't feel sociable, well, they didn't. But the twins usually did, and when he gave them a swift, shrewd look he saw they were far from being their normal selves. He could no longer have described Tom as 'a wonderfully good all-purpose boy'; his eyes were troubled and his usually rosy cheeks were pale. Pam, always pale, was now ashen, the expression in her eyes was tragic and her long, fair hair seemed to have less life in it than usual. Mike thought she now suggested not so much a child mermaid as a drowned child mermaid.

'Things not going well?' he enquired.

'Not uproariously,' said Tom.

'Like a chat, later?'

'A Midnight Oil Chat?' said Pam, a faint flicker of life in her eyes.

'Could be – if you don't mind waiting till late. I'm expecting one or two bad cases. But perhaps yours is a bad case?'

'*We* think so,' said Pam. 'But we don't mind waiting. Come on, Tom.' She turned away hastily, nervous in case the offer of a Midnight Oil Session would be whisked away. It offered some reason for living.

Mike looked after them speculatively. He had always considered their home life miraculously happy and been thankful for it. Really, the problems facing some of his pupils were hair-raising. He already knew that one of them had just returned from a home where a highly scandalous divorce was now a certainty. And another child had witnessed a wild scene of drug addiction. Rich people! Sometimes he thought he would never again take a child of rich parents – except that he could always overcharge rich parents which helped him to take children whose parents couldn't pay anything. Another child he would have to cope with tonight was a perpetual burner of his midnight oil – a girl who didn't like her psychiatrist. Mike wouldn't have liked him, either. He often longed to send away children who were taken to psychiatrists, but knew he would never have the heart to.

Mike was a slight, boyish-looking man in his middle thirties, with pleasantly untidy features and much admired red hair. He himself thought highly enough of this to get it set occasionally, to the ravishment of his pupils, male and female. But as it rarely stayed set for more than a few hours, he usually settled for keeping it very clean and letting it blow in the wind. His pupils thought pretty well of this, too.

Around mid-afternoon he was told the twins' grandmother was asking for him on the telephone.

'Hello, Gram,' he said, cheerfully. He had her amused permission to call her Gram. 'Well, tell me the worst. I can see there is one.'

She talked audibly and coherently, and he found everything so fascinating that he barely interrupted her. But when at last she said, 'Well, that's about all I can tell you,' he felt he must repeat to her the gist of all she had said to make quite sure he hadn't misunderstood anything. The whole story seemed so unlike the twins. He had of course known that Pam had a lively imagination, but he had never known her to confuse imagination with reality; and Tom was more apt to quell her flights of fancy, rather than support them. And both children were unusually truthful. Still, it did seem to him that they had been treating their adoring – and adored – grandmother to a series of invented incidents. If so, why?

He was impressed by Gram's own explanation. She had thought of various real-life happenings which might have overstimulated Pam's imagination. Very good detective work; it would be helpful when he confronted the twins. Gram also told him of Pam's early habit of telling her inventions as if they were true, and mentioned the tiger and the snake. 'And the fact that she did lie about the snake shows she *can* lie.' As for Tom, Gram was convinced he was lying just to support his sister and, Tom being the boy he was, he would never do that unless he had some overpoweringly good reason. *Was* Pam on the edge of a serious mental disorder?

Mike said he doubted it (actually it sounded to him as if Pam might be right in the middle of one). Anyway, it could all be sorted out as there was love on all sides. 'You love the twins and they love you. I love the twins and I think they're fond of me. Incidentally, I'm sure I should love you, too, given the chance. We must have a proper meeting, not just snippets of conversation at school parties.'

Gram, near tears with gratitude, said, 'I love you already, Mike. Please do remember I'll do *anything* you feel will help. I've forsworn myself and told them I believe them, but I don't think I convinced them. And I've *promised* I'll feed the kittens I don't believe exist. It was the last thing I said to them this morning. I said I'd wait up till midnight. Now I mustn't take up any more of your time.'

He assured her she'd been very welcome to it and that he'd ring her up next morning. 'Let's hope I can pour some of my midnight oil on troubled waters.' It was a joke that he made rather often and he was apt to worry in case he made it twice to the same person.

Late in the afternoon he intercepted the twins

as they came back from their walk and told them Gram had rung up. 'So I've got a sort of outline of things.'

'She *didn't* believe us, did she?' said Pam.

'Well, not *exactly.*'

'Did she say anything about the kittens?' said Tom.

'She's going to feed them, at midnight; that's good, isn't it? We'll talk it all out tonight. Don't come till ten and be prepared to wait. I've had another bad case wished on me.'

The new case, for once, involved the child of poor parents, who had taken to battering each other.

During their walk the twins had decided that, worried though they were about Gram's disbelief, what troubled them most was the fate of the kittens. Tom had been anxious about them from the beginning. Pam's anxiety had hit her with full force on the previous night. She felt less and less sure that magic would take care of them. Indeed, she felt less and less sure about magic. No one but her seemed to believe in it. Perhaps she couldn't keep it alive all on her own.

Somehow they got through the evening, got ready for bed at nine o'clock (dressing gowns were *de rigueur* for Midnight Oil Sessions) and met in the outer office of Mike's room at ten. A large jug of lemonade had been left for them, also some tempting books on which they were unable to concentrate.

It was long after eleven when Mike called them in, after ushering out a boy whose expression suggested tentative sunshine trying to break through after a long, wet day.

'Sit down,' said Mike, cheerfully. 'Like a drink?'

'Full up,' said Pam. 'I'm afraid we've drunk all your lemonade.'

'That's what it was there for. Waiting's thirsty work. Well, let's see if we can pour midnight oil –' He pulled himself up; not twice in one day. 'I wonder if you know how lucky you are, compared with many. Your gram's a wonderful woman and she loves you dearly.'

'We've been thinking that,' said Tom. 'It's extremely good of her to stay up till midnight when she must still be very tired, to feed kittens she doesn't believe are real.'

'And they really are real?'

The twins stared at him in momentary silence. Then Pam said, '*He* doesn't believe they are, Tom.'

'*Et tu, Brute*, Mike,' said Tom.

'Well quoted,' said Mike, without the suspicion of a smile. 'If it were only the kittens I'd believe without hesitation. But some of the other things, taken one after the other . . . Anyway, let me give you Gram's explanation of, well, er, everything. You told her that in Miss Freke's room at the nursing home there are lots of little pictures, some of them of animals. Gram thinks that one must have been of four kittens, and that put the idea into Pam's head.'

'Only we happened to see our kittens two days before we met Miss Freke,' said Tom.

'Ah. Well, let me go on with Gram's theory. She thinks you probably told Miss Freke about how you hunted for the secret room and she told you there really was one and, perhaps, how she found it. And then you imagined finding it. Gram says it was too late for you really to have gone to Freke Hall when you got home on Sunday night.'

'But I explained how we took the short cut across the fields,' said Pam.

'Which you knew would have been dead against her wishes. That's one reason she found it so hard to believe. And then, the squatters. She says you saw squatters on television on Saturday night.'

'Those were London squatters,' said Pam. 'And they didn't have babies in dresser drawers.'

'In dresser drawers?' Mike looked intrigued. 'That does seem a good place for them – except that one might shut them up and forget them.'

'Our squatters would never have done that. They were *nice* squatters,' said Pam, then added with cold courtesy, 'But please go on.'

He was finding it far from easy, confronted with two stony faces. 'Well, your gram was trying to put together all the things that might have, well, overstimulated Pam's imagination. And she remembers that, right from the beginning of the weekend, Pam was particularly imaginative. There was that plane which she thought might be a dragon. And then, when you were having supper by the fire that night – it did sound fun – you said how you resented the loss of magic, Pam, when you were told fairy tales weren't true. By the way, I didn't know until Gram told me today that, when you were younger, you used to say things were true when they weren't. Gram made me laugh about that tiger.'

'Did she mention the snake?' said Pam.

'I gather it was a genuine snake. I think Gram was shocked because you lied about it.'

'Only to save its life,' said Tom. 'I'd be proud to have that lie on my conscience.'

'Mike doesn't think any lies are excusable,' said Pam.

'I've never quite said that. Anyway, I'll say now that, as lies go, that was a pretty noble one. Perhaps you'll end up as St Pamela of All Snakes and we'll hold an All Snakes' Day.'

Grateful tears came into her eyes. 'Oh, Mike, how very kind of you – when I know how you feel about the Decay of Truth. I do try to be truthful. That's why it's so upsetting to have Gram believe I'm lying now.'

'She doesn't call it that. She just thinks your imagination's getting out of hand because you want to hang on to magic. She says you think the kittens are magical.'

'Only because they always came at midnight. Surely that must be magical?'

'Not necessarily. A mouse once turned up in my bedroom at one in the morning when I was still awake, reading. I put down a biscuit for it and, bless me, if it didn't arrive at exactly the same time the next night. It got another biscuit. And after that it came pretty well on the dot, for weeks and weeks. Animals have a strange in-built sense of time.'

'Sounds like magic to me,' said Pam. 'What happened to the mouse?'

'It eventually stopped coming.'

'Oh, dear.' Pam looked distressed. 'Can nothing be done about it?'

'I can hardly employ a mouse detective. Anyway, it was years ago. What we're discussing now is you. Honestly, Pam, it's time you gave up believing in magic.'

'Why?' said Tom, belligerently. 'She's as much right to believe in it as people have to believe in religion.'

'Anyhow, why should the little bit I said about magic make Gram believe I've made up a whopping series of lies? And what about Tom? He doesn't believe in magic, but he backed me up in everything I said.'

Mike looked at Tom very directly. 'Gram thinks

you've got some good reason for that – or what you think is a good reason. How about it, Tom?'

'I simply don't know what you're talking about,' said Tom. 'Do you, Pam?'

For a moment the twins looked at each other helplessly. Then Pam gave a gasp and cried, 'Oh, Tom! I've got my awful feeling – that I'm not here, not real. Oh, Tom, help me!'

'Just snap out of it,' said Tom. 'You know you always do, in a couple of minutes.' He turned to Mike. 'It's just that she sometimes gets a mad idea that she's just imagining herself and that if it goes on she won't, well, exist any more. But it never does go on. All right now, Pam?'

'I think so. Sorry, Mike. I know it doesn't make sense.'

'It does to me,' said Mike, 'because I sometimes felt it when I was a child. Not any more, though. I believe it can be the prelude to a mystical experience.'

'Not with me,' said Pam. 'Seeing that I'm an atheist.'

'Oh, pooh! Atheists often have mystical experiences.' Mike turned to Tom. 'Is this what's been frightening you? Have you been afraid she's going out of her mind? Is that why you've felt you must, well, back up all her imaginings?'

'No, no, no!' shouted Tom.

The vehemence of his tone alarmed Pam. She cried, 'Oh, Tom, have you been humouring me? *Have* I imagined everything?' Her voice rose hysterically.

And at that moment the telephone on Mike's desk rang. It startled Pam so much that she let out a scream, then toppled over the edge of hysteria.

Mike, grabbing the telephone, shouted to Tom, 'Stop her, stop her. If necessary, slap her.' Then he very angrily said, 'Hello!' on the telephone.

The voice he heard was high-pitched, excited, barely coherent; and as Pam's hysterics were continuing it was a full minute before he realised who was speaking. 'Oh, Mike – it *is* Mike, isn't it? I'm so sorry to ring you as late as this but I thought you'd still be up because of the Midnight Oil Sessions, and I wanted to make sure you'd tell the twins the very first thing in the morning. They're here!'

'They can't be,' said Mike, 'because they're here. What's where? What are you talking about? – Pam, shut up. It's your gram.'

Gram was still talking. 'And they came at midnight, just as the twins said. Suddenly, from nowhere, they were under the lilac tree.'

'Hang on a minute,' said Mike. 'Tom, grab the

extra earpiece and listen. Pam, when you get control of yourself, I'll hand over the telephone.'

She had stopped screaming and was merely sobbing. Now she gave one last gulp and rushed to Mike. He let her take the telephone and bent down beside her, still hearing much that Gram said.

At around half-past eleven she had put out food for the hedgehogs, watched unseen while they ate it and then put out more food. She was determined to keep her word to the twins and wait for the kittens until well after midnight.

Shortly before twelve Hildy returned from an evening in the village and came into the sitting room. She had told him nothing about her trouble with the twins and simply said now that she'd been feeding the hedgehogs. He joined her at the open french window just as midnight began to strike. Gram cast a quick glance into the moonlit orchard. No kittens.

'Came to tell you a bit of news,' said Hildy. 'Squatters have moved into Freke Hall.'

'What?' said Gram sharply, then gasped, 'Hildy, look! Under the lilac tree!'

They were there, all four of them, the white one, the black one, the ginger and the pale tabby. And now they were moving forward, coming closer and closer.

'And then they saw the food,' said Gram, 'and they *raced*, jostling each other to get at it. And I remembered, from all those years ago when Mogg was a stray kitten, that the way to make friends is to steal up behind them when they're eating, and then they associate the pleasure of eating with being stroked. And I ran out of the front door and sneaked up on them and managed to stroke them all. And tomorrow we'll coax them indoors – they'll be tame in no time at all.'

Tom grabbed the telephone from Pam. 'What's going to happen to them? You did say you wouldn't . . . get rid of them?'

Gram took a deep breath. 'I will keep them as long as I live and I will make provision for them, in my will, just as I did for Mogg. And I will never again disbelieve anything either of you say.'

'Oh, glorious Gram!'

Pam grabbed the telephone back. 'But can you afford it – when you're so inflated? Oh, perhaps we could give a cheese and wine party for them.'

'Darling, kittens don't like cheese and wine.'

'I meant in aid of them.'

Gram laughed. 'I won't quite need to do that.

Four tiny kittens won't ruin me, not even if they grow up to be enormous cats.'

'Sad we shan't see them while they're small,' said Pam.

Mike held up his hand. 'Tell her I'll drive you over one Sunday in a few weeks.'

While Pam relayed this he watched the renewal of vitality in her face. He also noticed there were tears of relief in Tom's eyes. The all-purpose boy had as much sensitivity as his sister. It was typical, Mike thought, that when Tom took the telephone for a last goodnight, his final words were to tell Gram to get herself a good night's sleep.

'She can't have had a real sleep for three nights,' he told Mike. 'Two nights nursing in the village and last night worrying about us. Poor darling Gram.'

'Did you hear everything she said?' asked Pam.

'Most of it, but you can tell me fully while we get something to eat. I bet you're both hungry now. We'll open up the kitchen.' He'd do scrambled eggs.

Gram, settling down to that good night's sleep Tom had told her to get, hoped she could lie awake long enough to luxuriate in thankfulness. She was particularly thankful that it had all been her fault. The twins were still just what they always had been

– the joy of her life. Distrusting them had felt like losing the basis of her existence. And she had been so baffled; they had seemed somehow to be ganging up against her. She hoped they would never know how deeply she had been troubled. And now there was so much to look forward to. Already she loved those four kittens for their own sakes. And mercifully Hildy had taken to them too. And earlier that day he had himself suggested that some of the flower beds should be grassed next year. It would mean an expense but, in the long run, a saving both of money and Hildy's time and labour. With care she could keep old Hildy happy and well for years yet.

And tomorrow she would see what she could do for the baby squatters. Hadn't Pam said they were being fed on cat food? Really, of all the fantastic stories, but Gram was now quite sure they were true. She suddenly remembered the Queen in *Alice in Wonderland* saying she had believed as many as six impossible things before breakfast. *Well, I'll do that, too,* thought Gram, *provided the twins tell me the impossible things.* And then, with babies in dresser drawers and kittens who presumably had an alarm clock which rang at midnight, for her to dream about, she drifted into sleep.

And the kittens? Little did they know that this was their last night in the small derelict rabbit warren where their mother had reared them.

Tomorrow they would sleep in a basket inherited from a famous cat called Mogg, which would later be supplied with a new cushion. And a cat door would soon be reopened for their use so that they could enjoy both the indoor and outdoor worlds. When the cow parsley was cut down, it would be found that, concealed in the roots of the great white lilac, there was a rabbit hole which was the back door of the warren. So there was no magic involved in their seeming appearance from nowhere. But they had experience of magic – when the touch of a hand had turned them from wild kittens into pet kittens, who would grow up to be pampered cats. As for why they always came at midnight? Well, if one could explain everything this would be a far less interesting world.